SPARED

A NOVELLA

OF FIRE AND SHADOWS

KRYSTA MARAVILLA

Published May 2023
krystamaravilla.com
Library of Congress TXu002373488

ISBN: 979-8-9874023-3-7 (e-book)

"Friendship and selfless support are what matters. These are the
priceless blessings in life that help us to overcome every difficult life
experience and life challenge."

—Lily Amis, *Leo & Mousi, Refugees Unwanted!*

CREDITS

Editor
Parisa Zolfaghari

Proofreader
Phoebe Zimmerer

Writing Platform
Bookcicle

Book Cover Design
Natasha MacKenzie

Writing Coach & Editor
Kelly Chausovsky

I've learned so much from each of you. From my heart space to yours,
Thank you.

READER ADVISORY

For the list of potentially triggering content,
please turn the page.

AUTHORS NOTE

Spared isn't a story I wrote lightly.

After years in mental health, I've sat beside survivors. I've seen how trauma reshapes a life—and how resilience, stitched from broken pieces, becomes something whole. Something fiercely beautiful.

This novella is for anyone carrying fear behind a mask. For those who feel trapped in their bodies and minds. For those haunted by a past they never asked for.

Spared doesn't promise escape—or easy answers. It's a chapter in Phe's journey—defined by persistence, courage, and the choice to keep moving, even when everything feels unfair, uncertain, and terrifying.

If this story leaves you with anything, I hope it's this: **You're not broken. You're not alone. Your story matters. Keep going.**

Stay marvelous,
—Krysta

ACKNOWLEDGMENTS

Oh seas! That was the fastest I have ever written anything to date, woot woot!! I'm over here giving myself high fives. The difference between the creation of Spark and this novella is radically and honestly, completely welcome. Thank goodness. To the thank you's!

Ever heard that being blessed with a creative family member or friend comes with its trials?

With me, I am often in my head. I prefer to be alone to craft, because interruptions and distractions pull me out of the zone. And when that happens, it's gone. I get anxious when I'm challenged with imagining scenes or creating dialogue. My family and friends take the brunt of all this cave hiding, pacing, intense communicating—you know, when you actually talk to like four people a week there's a lot to say—Nutella eating, and manifesting, and this feral author has eternal gratitude to each and every one of you.

One of the struggles I've had in my writing journey is finding a team of people who help my skills improve, one story at a time. So, it is with unbound excitement I get to thank everyone who was a part of this novella creation.

Kelly Chausovsky, I cannot truly express how deeply grateful I am to call you a friend and to have your support with all things writing and more. Parisa Zolfaghari, my editor, thank you for your patience with me and Elizabeth Thompson, I'm grateful for your manuscript assessment. Without all your feedback and edits, this story wouldn't be what it is. Natasha MacKenzie, is my book cover designer extraordinaire. This cover, like the rest in the series, is amazing.

My writing partner Pamela Hart—without you this road would be so much harder. I always look forward to our weekly meetings.

A special thanks to the NH Coalition Against Domestic and Sexual Violence, Meg and Alyssa, for speaking with me and providing information and resources for the afterword.

To my readers, thank you so much for reading my stories and investing your time and energy and money into them. I especially love when you reach out to tell me how the stories have touched you in some way or how you love Phe.

To every author, thank you for having the bravery to write and share your stories.

And, if you haven't heard it today, you are marvelous.

CONTENT WARNING

This novella contains references to:

- Violence
- Sex trafficking, human trafficking
- Sexual assault and abuse
- Kidnapping
- Coercion
- Mental health topics such as flashbacks, disassociation, and panic attacks.

1

The stiff leather restraints on Phe's wrists and ankles cut into her skin. Her pain had transformed into a dull ache that mimicked the steady, clunky movement of the wagon she'd been loaded into. The gag sawed into the edges of her lips, and the wet, lukewarm, heavy fabric transitioned to icy cold on her numb cheeks.

What in the world had she been thinking when she agreed to this?

Had she lost her mind? Had she forgotten the clawing panic that would ensue the moment they slapped those leather bands and cinched them tight? Had she overestimated her determination to overcome her fear when they'd shoved her into a barrel and sealed it? Had she not realized she'd be sentenced to the never-ending, heart-pounding darkness with even darker memories? Had she failed the mission when it hadn't even begun?

To be honest, Phe hadn't thought about any of those things—not her past, which hovered in the distance like a dark storm cloud, not her claustrophobia, not her aversion to touch. No. She hadn't thought about herself at all.

She'd thought about the abject abuse others were going through.

She'd thought about the lives that, from one heartbeat to the next, had their innocence shredded.

She'd thought about how no one should endure that type of abuse.

And she'd thought about how she could be a part of stopping it all.

Her stomach lurched with a sinking weightlessness for the second it took the barrel she was in to tip over and slam and roll and then forcibly stop. Pain unfurled from her head and shoulder and wrists and hip.

General Bastion had all of Shadow Unit, the elite military team Phe trained with, infiltrate the lower levels of an underground sex trafficking organization for months with no success. Thus, he'd requested her assistance with identifying the key players of the trafficking ring and using her sleuthing skills, when the opportunity arose, to search the premises of where she'd be held for any additional information, such as identities of trafficked victims, details on the ring's rumored auctions, where the victims were being held, and anyone who was involved—from the human traffickers to their clientele list.

General Bastion's goal was to send a very clear, severe, non-negotiable message. Xafara does not tolerate human trafficking of any sort. This message was to be conveyed by apprehending everyone taking part in the organization—ideally all at once—and handing them over to Xafara's legal system to do what it did best: publicly punish them.

What little information the members of Shadow Unit had gathered while undercover suggested that the head of the organization, who called himself the General, was obsessed with Lady Orphne. The General often took girls he thought resembled Lady Orphne for his own private use.

General Bastion had proposed Ihrone—who, along with all the other members of Shadow Unit, was undercover as a lowly sergeant in the trafficking organization—bring Phe to the General as a means to be promoted. General Bastion's hope was if Ihrone was in a higher position, he'd have access to the identities of those in his new status or above, gaining a deeper awareness of their trade routes, clients, and the inner workings of the organization.

With Phe's consent, General Bastion had arranged for her "kidnapping." She was transported with a small shipment of people to Oceanid—the hub of the organization—where Ihrone was to hand her over to the obsessed General.

This was Phe's first undercover mission.

The first mission where she wouldn't be the bringer of death, hidden in shadows.

The first mission where she must stay in her Lady Orphne persona and maintain it at all costs.

The heaviness of General Bastion's order weighed on her, for many reasons. Apprehension clogged her throat just considering having to endure the agony of touch—and that was simple contact. It was unknown what the General did with his girls, other than hushed rumors that he'd torture them for pleasure and discard the bodies. Yet, no bodies had been found.

What would he do to Phe?

Would she be able to submerge her warrior persona for the entirety of the mission?

Would she have flashes—where the memories of her violent past flooded into her present—and would they compromise the mission?

She worried about her flashes because she could never predict how she'd react in one. Sometimes, they passed by so quickly, it was disorientating. Other times, she lashed out blindly—which was what she was petrified of. If she were to attack, her training and skill would be hard to overlook.

Would her past take this opportunity to seize the reins?

What would she do if the General tried to hurt her or touch her inappropriately?

How could she stop him if she couldn't break cover from her Lady Orphne persona?

Would this mission shred all the work she'd done to heal from her time with Grum?

Phe angled her bound wrists to scratch her chest and shoulder, ignoring the dried filth that bunched up under her nails. These last few questions she didn't want to think about at all because the only thing she could do was survive, one moment at a time. As she had done before she met Kyra—her best friend and the last Water Nymph in all of Aethra who protected the waterways of Xafara, their island country, and the reason Phe lived a dual life—when she was with Grum, her childhood abuser and Shalexum—a country from the mainland—owner.

Gads, why did I agree to this?

The barrel was wrenched upright. Muffled noises breached the barrel's walls, the first sounds she'd heard in about two days.

She had agreed because of the victims . . . Because she knew what it felt like to be treated as a possession. To be forced to do things and to survive brutal beatings because of her status.

Phe pressed her face into the wood, finding the small opening Ihrone had cut out for air. Her throat was drier than a desert, having lost its moisture to the gag. Seas, was she thirsty.

It was a good thing no one expected her to come out of this barrel fighting, because there was no way she could've. Not after roughly two days in this stinking, cramped, misery-infused space.

This torture? It's only the appetizer, a mere sample of what's promised, she reminded herself. *But in this story, I am not a child.* She went over this with herself as much as she could to combat the fear that this would be the mission that broke her.

Grimly, she knew Elzac—the man who saved her during her Drykz Forest incident and taught her to be aware of her thoughts and how they powered her—would be proud of her. Proud of her for reminding herself she was not a perpetual victim, and that she was the narrator of her own life story. *In this story, I am powerful,* she added for good measure, even though it didn't feel like it.

The wood shuddered under the aggressive thunk-thunk of someone prying the lid off. Within seconds, the lid lost its seal, and a chaotic jumble of sounds speared her senses.

Gads, she missed Elzac and Ligeia—the hidden village within

Drykz Forest. Life had been much simpler there. The village was a protective, hidden bubble amid the deadly forest.

Calloused hands reached in and grabbed her face, torquing her chin up. Immediately, the skin-to-skin contact rippled with burning pain that seized her lungs, her aversion to touch—remnants from Grum's physical abuse—triggered. The throbbing of her head increased exponentially.

She felt Ihrone's shadow lean over the now open barrel but couldn't bring herself to pry open her eyes. Not yet.

"It's me," Ihrone breathed, brushing aside sticky, crusty hair from her face.

Air filled her lungs.

It tasted of sea, tinged with pungent decay, and blended with sweat.

They were near the ocean.

Ihrone's nimble fingers went to work on releasing the gag. Louder, he said, "I'm taking this off, but make a sound . . ." He let the silence complete his threat and brought a bottle to her mouth, letting drops of water wet her lips. "Drink."

She did, flooding the barren wasteland of her parched mouth. How long had it been since she'd had water? Eaten?

"What's that smell?" someone exclaimed.

"It's Lady Orphne," Ihrone replied while he drizzled more water into her mouth, giving her a few small sips that barely quenched her thirst. He poured the rest onto her face and neck, followed by a wet rag that came away caked in brown sludge, sludge that Phe refused to think about. Then Ihrone hauled her out of the barrel, not ungently.

"High Seas!" someone exclaimed past Ihrone's shoulder. "Is that really her?"

"Who knows?" another strange male voice responded. Phe hated both their voices. "Could be one of her lookalikes." Then he jeered, "Who'd have thought Lady Orphne would have so many?"

Another laughed condescendingly. "She doesn't. Have you seen the ones coming through? If they have chestnut brown hair or eyes even close to honey colored, that's it. He takes them."

"It sure looks like the reports of her," the first guy said. "Olive skin, chestnut brown hair, petite, and did you see the amulet she's wearing?" Giddy excitement spiked the man's last words. "Why is she so filthy?"

Ihrone didn't answer.

Phe ignored them, too focused on funneling strength into her weak legs, breathing clean air, and not thinking about why General Bastion insisted she be coated in sewage. Still, Phe's legs crumpled like limp octopus tentacles the moment Ihrone set her on her feet, and the restraints at her ankles dug into her. Ihrone's bruising grip was the only reason she didn't face-plant.

"Mmmmm," Ihrone muttered noncommittally, swinging Phe into his arms and cradling her to his chest. The new position puckered her skin. Phe automatically stiffened and leaned away from him. Ihrone readjusted, tucking her tighter. "Tell Lieutenant Grey I won't be handing her over to him. It's only the General himself if he wants her."

Phe gritted her teeth against waves of body-locking discomfort. She squinted and scanned her surroundings, finding an array of greedy, calculating gazes locked onto her. Beyond them, the room was tight with the barrels lining one side of it and cases of liquor on the other. The small portions of wall she could see were dirty, with splotches suggesting water damage.

"No one knows you here." A scruffy man edged closer. "It'd be best if we take—"

Ihrone scoffed condescendingly. "You heard me. I've got *his* girl. If he wants her, he has to come get her."

The man guffawed with laughter. It was hoarse and arrogant and sent shivers of revulsion along the ladder of her spine. Phe wanted to punch him. Instead, she clenched her fists so tightly, her nails pierced her palms and the leather restraints burrowed into her flesh. "You're crazy," the man said.

Ihrone shrugged as if he didn't have a care in the world and wasn't facing off with a half dozen ruthless, power-hungry bottom feeders. "Call me what you like. I'll be in my room taking *care* of her."

The implication of how he was going to take care of her swept stillness into the room.

Someone cleared his throat. "The General doesn't take kindly to others playing with his girls."

Ihrone snorted and left the room, striding casually through narrow, filthy hallways of what Phe deduced was a brothel. Yet Phe felt the readiness of his muscles as he held her. It was only when he'd heel-kicked a door shut and propped her on a rickety chair that some of his tension appeared to ebb.

"Phe, there's time to back out," Ihrone said, worry etched into the lines of his face as he crouched a few feet in front of her. "You don't have to do this. We can find another way."

Confined by her restraints, Phe two-handedly brushed knotty hair from her face. She cleared stagnate phlegm, saliva, and fear from her throat. "No." The cracks at the corners of her mouth zinged. "I can do this." *I have to. I have to save these victims. I have to help.*

Ihrone didn't look convinced, the wrinkles deepening around his eyes. "We know nothing about the General other than his fixation on you. The rest is rumors, but with this crowd, I don't doubt there is truth to them."

Phe pointed and flexed her toes, the movement causing a rush of pain up her legs from the abrasion caused by the restraint on her ankles. She knew the pretenses of this mission; she had no illusions. General Bastion had told her the details they knew.

Phe knew this mission was going to test her. Test her ability to tolerate touch—and who knew what level of depravity the General would inflict on her. Test her ability to stay in her Lady Orphne persona, only switching to her warrior one when she wouldn't be at risk of breaking cover. And it was going to test all her inner cracks to see if they held.

Will this be the test that finally shatters me? That thought gave her pause. With her past and her aversion to touch and—she shook herself. She couldn't go down that path. No matter what, the mission was going to affect her. It was a fact, but it didn't deter her from the mission. Not when others' lives were at stake.

She chewed on Ihrone's comment for a moment and then forced out. "Are you saying I'll fail?"

"No." Ihrone's steady, concerned gaze never flickered. "Not at all. I'm saying, with your past, this will be extremely difficult."

Even though Phe had never shared her past prior to her friendship with Kyra, she knew Shadow Unit suspected something terrible had happened. Her extreme aversion to touch and reluctance to speak more than necessary, eight years later, were signs even the most unaware person would notice, and the members of Shadow Unit were definitely not unobservant.

Phe smiled, barring her teeth. "I can kill him at any time, right?"

"You can."

But killing was a last resort. Even though Phe could kill easily, it was something she did only on orders from General Bastion. And, unlike all her other missions, killing the General was not what they wanted.

Killing the head of the organization wouldn't send the right message.

Phe grunted, done with the conversation. She had accepted this mission, and she was going to see it through.

"If things get too bad, I'm just a thought away," Ihrone said in his reassuring, fatherly way.

Phe scrunched her nose. What did that mean? Nothing. If things got bad, he wouldn't be there to rescue her.

Heavy footsteps sounded in the hallway.

"I ordered a meal when I secured the room," Ihrone said, somehow knowing what she was going to ask before she'd even opened her mouth. He was always doing that. His perceptive abilities were one of the many ways Ihrone amazed her. The wood floor creaked as Ihrone crossed it, meeting the person at the door. Sure enough, the heavenly scent of food tickled her senses. Whatever it was, the cook had been heavy-handed with garlic.

Phe'd instinctively scanned the nondescript room when they'd entered, but with Ihrone no longer monopolizing her gaze, she soaked it all in. A queen-sized wood frame held an old, well-used mattress covered with thin, patchy blankets. Curtains that appeared to not have been washed in the last decade covered the single window, where stains of red-brown and dirty cream and dark browns —of who knew what—were covered in dust.

"Phe." Ihrone dropped the food on the wobbly wood frame masquerading as a table next to her. The table tottered to the left, and the stew sludged over the rim, puddling at the bowl's ceramic base. "You don't have much time. They'll be here soon. Eat."

Phe glanced sharply at him. Seas, she needed more time.

She swallowed, her bone-dry throat clicking against itself, clawing for moisture. It scraped, struggled, and scoured the length of her throat, the entire snail's crawl to the empty pit of her stomach.

Her belly seized the moment to growl, pulling her from the dread that had pooled and congealed like the stew had on the table.

She gathered her flimsy courage and faced off with the steaming stew. Wrapping both bound hands around the bowl, she brought it to her mouth and slurped the viscous, garlic-ladened medley with its chunks of stringy, chewy meat.

The clunking of several sets of heavy footsteps clambered down the hallway, accompanied by mutterings.

Phe locked Ihrone in her stare but didn't stop shoveling the stew. Even though her stomach knotted painfully, trepidation cinching the massive knot tighter, she didn't know when she'd get her next meal.

Those gray, worried eyes of Ihrone's captured hers briefly before he stood and unsheathed one of his thigh knives while he strode to the door.

Gads, what am I doing? Fear electrified her nerves. A torrent of panic lunged and jabbed at her, only to be backhanded by her determination.

She'd never failed a mission before, and she wouldn't fail this one. Not when an untold number of lives depended on her.

The steps pounded toward them.

Calmly, she put the soup spoon down.

The footsteps stopped outside the door.

Taking a steadying breath, Phe channeled her Lady Orphne persona, letting whisps of terror curl her shoulders. She pressed both fists to her mouth, letting the fear creep back in slightly. But only slightly.

It was showtime.

2

The door started to burst open, but it slammed into Ihrone, who barricaded the doorway.

"Ompf!" cried the man trapped in the crack between Ihrone, the door, and the frame.

Ihrone bashed the pommel of his knife into the man's temple. The man slumped, limply, stuck in place.

"I'll kill every single one of you," Ihrone grunted, his body blocking their entry. "Starting with this one."

Phe bit into the joints of her fingers. *This was it.* Her thighs, though covered in ridiculous layers of filthy petticoats, felt naked without her leather sheaths and the comforting weight of her knives.

Gads, she wished they could kill them now. Wished the mission was that easy.

"Stop!" commanded a male voice. A voice that was semi-familiar to Phe. "There's no need for violence."

Shock slapped Phe, and a veil of apprehension descended. If there was a thread of familiarity, it meant he was a part of Kyra's social circle, which included the royal family, parliament, and all the influential families within Xafara. It meant she and Kyra had spent time with them and, possibly, whoever else was part of this organization, and that made everything worse. It's one thing to investigate strangers, but knowing even one of them brought the heinousness of what they were doing even closer to home.

"Then you should've knocked politely," Ihrone chided, grunting as the door vibrated from another impact.

"Point taken," the same voice conceded, then called off his men. "We're here for the girl."

Phe scoured her memory, trying to place the voice.

"I'll only release her to the General," Ihrone said into the wood panel, his tone non-negotiable.

"So I've heard," the man said casually, though disdain edged his tone. "I do not answer to others, so she better be the real thing."

Her heart rammed into the confines of her chest, threatening to explode. *The General is here.* Her skin tingled uneasily, and her mind went blank. Completely empty.

"Sheathe your weapons," Ihrone demanded, "and if anyone tries any funny business, I'll kill all of you."

Seas, this is it.

Phe's breaths came in short, shallow puffs around her fists. Why did she have to recognize his voice? Recognizing his voice suddenly made this so much harder.

Who would fixate on me so much they collected girls that looked like me and did untold things to them? What will he do to me?

"Fine," was spat in response.

Ihrone didn't move, nor did he say anything. After a long moment, the man grumpily said, "We're waiting."

"I am too," Ihrone responded. "Waiting on your men to sheathe their weapons."

Again, there was a heavy pause. How Ihrone knew they hadn't sheathed their weapons was one of his superpowers—if people had superpowers.

Ihrone abruptly released the door, his strides ravenously eating the distance between the door and Phe. The man at the door thudded to the floor, and six others stepped over him, eyeing Ihrone.

Phe's stomach twisted. The garlic threatened to burn its way free of her belly.

Ihrone grabbed the tangled mess of hair at her nape, cranked her head roughly, and exposed her neck. Her hands dropped to her lap and she became statue still. The cold, sharp point of his knife nicked her.

Phe gasped. Her pulse throbbed against the knife's rigid edge.

Five of the men were people she'd seen downstairs. Bottom feeders. Grasping greedies.

The last two were different. Phe could almost smell their cleanliness. Their clothes were not the simple garments the others wore but fine pieces of craftsmanship, with needlepoint precision and—Phe had no doubt—the best quality material. From the tips of their shining shoes to their glistening styled hair, they were the embodiment of Oceanid's elite society.

Their faces were covered in full decorative masks, showcasing only their eyes. One man had dark brown eyes with a multi-colored mask, resembling a peacock, while the other had green eyes and a solid black mask with horns protruding from his temples.

"Hurt her and you're a dead man." Menace punched each word, and it came from *that* voice. Phe's gaze flicked to the mask filled with color. The peacock.

"Let's get some things straight." Ihrone's grip on Phe's hair relaxed as he spoke, but the knife never left her skin. "I don't plan on hurting her unless you make me. Are you going to make me?"

One of the gasping greedies cleared his throat, breaking the silence.

Ihrone seemed to interpret that as an agreement. "I said I'd only release her to the General. Who are you?"

"You've garnered the attention of the General *and* his colonel," the horned-masked man informed them as his gaze seesawed between Ihrone and Phe. "Are you claiming *this* is Lady Orphne?"

"I am."

Six sets of eyes settled on Phe, their prying gazes trying to see past her mangled hair, dirt caked skin, and soiled dress.

"She's filthy," the horned man said with a disgusted sneer. "I can smell her from here."

Phe tried to hide her face and earned herself a deeper cut.

"Show me her wrist," Peacock demanded, skewering her with a gaze that attempted to scrub the grime from her.

"You heard the man," Ihrone said, shaking her head when she hadn't moved.

Phe lifted her hands. The fabric that had covered her arms drooped to her elbows, exposing her unique wrist amulet.

"It's her," Peacock whispered in awe.

Horned man glanced at Peacock and muttered, "Could be a replica piece." To Ihrone, his tone turned cold and speculative. "How were you able to take her from her guard?"

"I'm good at what I do." The blade at Phe's throat bobbed with Ihrone's shoulder shrug. "Let's talk about my reward."

Horned man scoffed. "You mean your demands?"

Ihrone dug the tip further into her flesh.

Phe hissed and squinted her eyes, not needing to exaggerate her grimace. It hurt. Warm blood trickled to her collarbone.

"No need to be dramatic." Peacock held up a hand, and that was the moment Phe deduced he, and not the horned man, was the General. "We want Lady Orphne." Peacock paused, then tacked on. "Alive. This is unprecedented for us, that's all."

"Well, tell your lackey here to back off. I don't like his attitude," Ihrone snapped. His grip tightened and threatened to pull out clumps of Phe's hair.

Phe gritted her teeth, gnashing her pain and frustration and fear together. If only they could capture these men now. Interrogate them until they revealed everything Shadow Unit needed to dismantle the organization.

She dragged in an aggrieved breath.

They couldn't risk it. Couldn't take the chance these two men would hold their silence about the organization, allowing the operation to continue. Something about the way the two Oceanid elitists held themselves told her it was a strong possibility.

"What is it you'd like, Curo?" the General asked. "Your name's Curo, right?"

"Yes, and I'd like a promotion." Ihrone rested the blade on her shoulder, easing the tip from her flesh.

"To what level?" the General asked as sharply as his gaze.

"Captain, sir."

"Aren't you cocky?" Contempt dripped heavily from the Colonel's voice.

Rather than responding, Ihrone dragged the knife down Phe's neck.

Phe bit her lip.

"Stop," Peacock ordered.

Ihrone did. "What did I say about his attitude?"

The two masked men exchanged looks. The Colonel shrugged and stepped back. Peacock took a step forward.

"Within our organization, there are specific ways you earn promotions. What you've done," the General's voice was severe, "we consider rogue behavior. It could bring unwanted attention to the organization. Yet . . . I find myself willing to make an exception."

"How does all of Xafara not know she's been taken?" the Colonel asked, hands resting on his weapons.

"How am I to know?" Ihrone loosened his grip. "Maybe they're relieved she's gone—you know, with how everyone feels about her."

Phe rolled the fabric of her dress, ignoring the stabbing pain Ihrone's words caused. Why did it matter that everyone hated her? Everyone, that is, except Kyra, Jallia (Kyra and Phe's maidservant), and the Royal family of Xafara. She wasn't there to be the most popular or to be liked. Yet the throbbing wound in her chest didn't seem to have gotten the message.

"Hmm. Her Grace must not know, or else all of Xafara would be up in arms searching for her." The General's eyes fixed unwaveringly on Phe. "I'm sure they're searching for her. Unwilling to let Her Grace know about their failure just yet."

"I don't like it," the Colonel stated, his tone portraying the scowl his mask hid.

"You don't have to," the General chided, flicking his intense gaze to Ihrone.

"You've had her for how many days and there hasn't been an announcement she's missing?"

"Going on three days, sir."

The General cocked his head to the side, his slimy gaze coating Phe. "How good are you at covering your tracks?"

Ihrone's voice smiled. "Even better than kidnapping people, sir."

The General bobbed his head. "From what I've heard of you, Curo, that's impressive."

"You'll understand, then, that being a foot soldier isn't enough for me. I'm seeking to grow under your tutelage."

"Coercing a jump in rank is not the best way to obtain this, but I recognize we haven't given you any other options. And you did acquire a priceless possession I've only dreamed of having."

"General . . ." the Colonel said in warning tones. The General ignored it.

"Curo, you have your promotion." The General strode across the room to loom over Phe, unconcerned with his proximity to Ihrone and his knife. "Colonel, please assign him a crew. Curo, you report directly to him—good luck. If this meeting is anything to go by, he's not a fan." The General's gaze bore into Phe. "Now, leave. You're no longer needed."

Ihrone's knife disappeared, as did the grip on her hair.

The General leaned into Phe's space and grabbed her by the nape, pulling her face closer to his.

Her lungs deflated, refusing to suck in air, and shadows poured into the edges of her vision. The peacock mask blurred, and his dark brown eyes drained to Grum's lighter brown. She yanked her head away, trying to dislodge his grip, but he held on tighter.

The skin-to-skin contact instantly caused flares of pain that ravaged her neck and arrowed into her head. Agony immediately speared her.

He's not Grum. Grum's dead. He's not Grum. She fought the encroaching panic.

The mask the General wore moved, probably from the delighted smile Phe could see awakening in the depths of his gaze.

"I've been waiting a long time for you, Orphne." His thumb tenderly circled her neck, and his eyes glittered with excitement and anticipation. "We're going to have so much fun getting to know each other."

Seas, this was going to suck.

3

Phe flicked her gaze to Ihrone's back, silently pleading. *Don't leave me. Don't leave me.* Whatever hope she'd bundled into her plea sunk to the pit of her stomach when he disappeared into the hallway without a glance at her.

Gads. If only Ihrone could have heard her mental cry. *I'm so—*

The General released her neck, dragging his hand across her flesh to cup her cheek, tearing her from her thought. Scalding pain erupted, branding her tense jaw.

"Cripes, she smells," the Colonel griped, his tone petulant and unhappy. "What'd he do, roll her in manure?"

Phe blinked and dipped her gaze to the white knuckles of her clasped hands peeking through the layer of brown filth covering her. That wasn't exactly what she'd rolled in, but it was close. She'd lost her ability to smell herself about a half hour into her barrel ride— thank the stars. It appeared the time in the barrel had only ripened her scent.

"Oh, Orphne," the General cooed menacingly, his agonizing touch caressing her jawbone. "You must be so scared."

Phe slowly sucked air in for four counts. Each count forced her constricted lungs to expand a millimeter, barely enough room for a shallow breath.

"Soldiers, return to your tasks," the Colonel snapped. "Make sure all our product's been loaded. We'll be leaving immediately." Footsteps bounded from the room, only to stop when the Colonel added, "And someone take this imbecile with you."

From Phe's periphery, she watched the last two men grab the unconscious man and haul him up between them, dragging him from the room.

"Did he *touch* you?" The General's voice steeled and his grip on her chin tightened, forcing her to focus on him.

Phe got the distinct impression that if she said yes, the General would send every soldier he had after Ihrone. She clamped her mouth shut, shaking her head no.

"Hmph." The General stepped to her side and wrapped his torturous hand around her bicep, pulling her up as he uttered, "Stand."

The restraints on her wrists and ankles dug into her raw, chafed skin. Her dress brushed against the rickety table. It wobbled, like her legs did before she locked her knees in place.

"Pity he didn't," the Colonel noted, leaning on the doorframe and crossing his arms. "Maybe that's why he dragged her through sewage?"

The General snorted. Phe felt his gaze skim her from head to toe, assessing.

It reminded her exactly of—no, she wasn't going to think about that. Not the daily beatings Grum would inflict when her silent presence inevitably angered him or when she displeased him. Not the times Grum had dragged her, beaten and starved and filthy, to the arenas. She wasn't going to think about how boys and girls had circled her in the Fyerir Fights, taking their measures of a scrawny seven-year-old girl and placing bets on her life. Nope. She wasn't going to think about it.

Yet . . . this felt oddly similar. Like Grum circling and assessing her. And it held vestiges to when she was forced into an arena to fight and, like her Fyerir fighting days, she wasn't sure she'd survive.

The General strode forward. His unrelenting hold on her arm lurched her torso toward him, and Phe toppled like a falling tree, crashing into the General's side.

Phe hissed.

The General grunted.

Instead of slamming into the floor, she hung limply above it, partially on the General's leg. She was so close to the ground, she could make out the granules of dirt, the imperfections of the wood, and see its wear pattern.

Her left arm—the one the General held—was cranked awkwardly, twisting her into him. Her wrist restraints burrowed deeper into her, pain shooting up her arm to match the torture of the General's touch.

The Colonel loudly sniffed. "Gads, she's a mess," he unhelpfully stated.

"He must have bound her legs," the General huffed, ignoring the Colonel's comment.

Her view blocked by the General, Phe heard the Colonel push off the wall and head to them. With a put-upon sigh, he muttered, "I'll help."

"I got her," the General snapped, half-righting Phe.

Instead of trying to stand, Phe flailed to keep a distance from her and the General's body. Being pressed against him sent jitters of repulsion coursing through her. The General heaved her to her feet, the mask partly twisting to the side of his face as his hands steadied her.

The Colonel's steps didn't stop.

"I said—"

"Oh, calm down," the Colonel said dismissively. He kept his face tilted away from Phe as he crouched at her feet. "I've got the restraints." An icy hand grasped her ankle, while the other flipped the layers of petticoats up. Phe felt both hands working to release her. "Not sure why you didn't just let her drop. It'd have been easier."

A flood of searing pain climbed Phe at his contact, and she lost the fight to control her shudder.

"Did you feel that?" The Colonel worked quickly, unfastening them. "She's so reactive, I can almost smell her fear over the stench. I can't wait for us to play with her."

The General ground his teeth.

The Colonel slid away from her as fast as he could. "I don't know how you can stand to be that close."

The moment the restraints were gone, blood pounded into her deprived feet. Throbbing superseded the flash of relief at the loss of the Colonel's touch.

"It's hard. I'll give you that." The General shrugged, his frustration with the Colonel seeming to evaporate with the movement. "But you know how long I've waited to touch her." He started walking again, leading them into the hallway. This time Phe kept up, barely. Her feet were pincushions of pins and needles.

How long has he wanted to touch me? Her heart wrapped itself in a big hug and began to rock. *What does he plan to do?*

"I know." The Colonel's tone emitted a vibe of deflated patience and trailed off behind them.

Phe's heart pounded like a manic woodpecker. *Why me?* she wondered, stumbling along beside the General. *What caused the General to fixate on me?* Her thoughts only made the mess of her heart shake more.

"Isn't it a good thing I insisted Willa come with us?" the General continued.

This was the worst idea, she berated herself, trying—and failing—to gulp air. *Ever.*

"You're not riding with them?" The Colonel's voice dropped subtly, leaving his statement hanging in a question.

"Gads, no. I enjoy breathing." The grip on her arm tightened painfully—as if the thought of letting her go made him tightfisted—cutting off the blood flow.

A wave of relief swept through her even as more pain blossomed where he held tight to her.

Thank the stars General Bastion ordered me to roll in dung. Phe blinked repetitively. She'd thought he'd done it to be a bastard—and let's be honest, he was being one—but now? If it gave her a reprieve from her upcoming fate . . .

Nope.

There was no way the small reprieve she was about to get would overshadow the fact that General Bastion had her dragged through dung and dirt and who knows what else before she was restrained and sealed in a barrel, where she then marinated in all of it. For two excruciating days. He didn't deserve thanks. He deserved a punch in the face.

"We can't follow closely either," the Colonel said firmly, the hint of uncertainty gone from his voice. "In fact, we should be seen tonight."

The General jerked her hard. "No—"

Phe tripped. Her body crashing into the silk fabric and hard planes of the General's body again—though this time she turned her shoulder into him—cutting off whatever else he was going to say.

"Ugh," burst from the General at the contact.

A burst of shrill laughter sounded through the thin wall to her left, and a rhythmic pounding—most likely a headboard slamming into the wall—started.

A clump of her hair smacked her face. Phe's whole body cringed.

"Your suit's ruined." Disgust dripped like a slowly melting icicle from the Colonel's words. "And I liked that one."

The General hauled her upright, uncaringly, and grunted. "I'll get a new one."

Cool, briny air blasted Phe in the face when the Colonel pushed open a door.

They spilled into the area where she'd been unloaded. A glancing sweep showed the neat row of stacked barrels lined up against the wall. Phe counted seven before the General yanked her out a door and into an alley. She knew this alley. They'd exited from the Final Swallow, one of Madam Wren's less-refined brothels.

The dank alley merged onto Grafton Street—a street Phe was all too familiar with from her nightly runs—where carriages lined the sidewalks as far as Phe could see.

This, General Bastion had told her about.

They employed the shell game: hiding people in a carriage and using a fleet of other carriages to confuse those who tracked them. It was a tactic they used successfully.

A severe-looking woman stood in front of a carriage, the only one with its door open. Gray laced her brown hair, which was pulled into an ultra-tight bun at the back of her head. She wore a conservative, black dress. Its neckline, which appeared more like a collar to Phe, stopped at the woman's sharpened chin. Her eyes were so dark, Phe at first thought they were black until the woman lanced her with them. Dark brown.

"Willa," the General said, greeting her.

The woman gave him a sharp nod, not shifting her shrewd gaze. "Sir."

"I hope you have a strong stomach," the Colonel called from the head of the carriage, where he'd strode to and was talking to the driver.

A spindly hand rose to cover the woman's nose. "Sir. If you would permit, once we have her in the carriage, I can strip her to her petticoats. Or we can clean her here."

Phe dropped her gaze.

"No time. You can take off her dress, but we don't have time to clean her. She goes as she is."

"Yes, sir." Without another word, Willa reached for Phe. Her gangly fingertips dug into the tender flesh of Phe's tricep—searing into Phe like a set of branding probes—her mouth puckered. "Get in," she ordered coldly.

The General released his hold, and Phe scrambled into the carriage. Willa followed.

"Sir, give me two minutes to undress her, please."

Phe froze in the middle of the cramped space, immediately noticing the covered windows. The plush bench seating, the cushioned walls, the small, uncovered window to communicate with the driver, and—conveniently—a folded blanket. Willa's presence loomed behind her, beaming hostility.

The walls pulsed, closing in on her.

Phe closed her eyes, and both hands gripped the skirt of her filthy dress. At one point, this silk dress had been a striking navy blue. Now, you couldn't see the color. Not with all the filth that caked it.

"Willa, do you need help?" the Colonel asked. Phe's eyes flew open, and she twisted to peer at the doorway, where he had appeared.

"Absolutely not," the General said, grabbing the Colonel's arm to stop him from getting in. "I thought you were disgusted."

"I am, *but* . . ." The Colonel trailed off, and Phe couldn't fathom what he was insinuating.

"No." The General shook his head. Whatever it was the Colonel left unsaid, he knew and didn't like. "Willa, you are the only person allowed to care for her. Do you understand? No one else can see her."

"Yes, sir," the woman responded, her voice devoid of emotion. "If you could give me a moment, sir?"

Phe looked into the woman's eyes. Eyes devoid of anything except Phe's own wide-eyed stare. The door closed, sealing in the stench and the darkness. Phe's stomach churned.

Willa's fingers started working on the buttons at the back of Phe's dress. Within seconds, her dress was off, and the soulless woman wrapped her and the remaining wreckage of petticoats into the blanket. "Sit."

Not peeling her gaze from the woman, Phe crammed herself into a corner seat.

Willa cracked the door open, sticking her head out. Once it appeared she'd gotten the all-clear, she handed the ruined dress out.

The General commanded someone to burn it before fixing his attention on Phe's bundled form. As his shrewd gaze took her in, Phe shrunk into the seat as far back as she could go, as if the shadows could hide her.

Without taking his eyes off Phe, he said, "Willa." The chill in the General's voice had Willa flashing him a wary glance. "Ready her to be presented to me."

"Yes, sir."

The vile weight of the General's gaze dropped to her shoulders then blazed a trail down the length of her body. Gooseflesh rose all over her, in sickly, prickly ripples. "Guard her with your life, because if she escapes, it will be forfeit, along with all of your family's lives."

"Yes, sir." The woman's voice came out strong, but her hands trembled.

"She will reside in the golden room."

"Yes, sir."

"From now on, you are her constant companion. The only time you leave her side is when she's with me." The General twisted his head, and Phe got the impression he was glaring in the Colonel's direction. "No one else."

Phe dragged in a breath. Investigating with a bulldog guard who was likely to lock her in a room and shepherd her with aggressive growls and nips if she tried to wander off was problematic. *How am I going to do what they sent me in to do?*

"Yes, sir." This time, Willa swallowed. Without anything further, the General closed the door and called to the drivers.

It was Phe's turn to gulp, and she slammed her eyes shut. If she didn't see the walls crowding her, then she'd be fine. *One problem at a time.* She tried swallowing again, pushing past the resurrection of garlic and stringy meat in her throat.

I'm doing this for the victims.

"Move, and I will stab you," Willa hissed, leaning into Phe's face, her breath warm and nasty. Once she was comfortable across from Phe, Willa pulled out a knife and left it on her lap.

Phe kept her gaze lowered, chin tucked into her neck and the blanket. The clawing panic that kept her chest tight and her heart racing cinched its grip and stole her breath.

Seas, don't let me fail.

The carriage lurched with the neighing of horses. Many, many horses.

4

"Stop," Willa ordered, pinching Phe's arm like a nasty dog nipping at its prey.

Shivers of fresh pain thrummed to life along Phe's nerve endings, zinging through her veins. Her skin was raw and flushed from Willa's scrubbing. It had taken several bathwater changes to ensure her cleanliness. Phe had track marks of bristles from the brush Willa had used on her body, hundreds of raw scrapes that didn't react well to the corset Willa then crammed Phe into or the texture of the new petticoats.

Somewhere between the long carriage and the third brutal bath scrubbing, Phe's heart had stopped rocking and she'd poured all her focus into watching Willa.

The woman had remained statuesque throughout the carriage ride; even her gaze had remained fixed—staring intently at Phe—knife gripped tight, her face set into a permanent sour pucker.

The hours they'd spent together, thus far, Willa had only barked orders at her. Her touch had been harsh and painful and deliberate, inciting an inferno of all-encompassing pain. Phe quickly understood Willa was a woman of minimal words—which Phe appreciated—and efficient. So efficient, Phe deduced Willa had done this before . . . many, many times.

Tucking her arms as close to her sides as possible to make herself smaller, Phe scanned the opulent room surrounding her. Willa had stopped next to the shiny sleigh bed in the middle of the room. Directly opposite it, glass doors opened onto a wide, curved balcony that reached past her sight and around the building. The walls were painted a beautiful golden color, and the delicate, exquisite rugs matched precisely.

"Eyes down. Stay," Willa commanded, as if Phe were a dog. The woman strode across the room to a wall with a built-in bookshelf, stacked with brightly-bound books, and disappeared through a door. A fireplace book-ended the shelving, and several seats surrounded it.

Phe slid clammy hands down the lines of her gold-colored silk dress, acutely aware of the missing weights of her knives. Her wrists protested with the movement. The open wounds at the base of her palms, bright pink with streaks of darker red, were so sensitive the air hurt.

Phe swung her gaze to the balcony doors and peered into the darkness. The only lights she saw were the twinkling of stars. Phe knew what it was like to be in Willa's position—albeit she'd been a child at the time—which left her warring between compassion for Willa and dislike. It was during those years of Phe's childhood that her intolerance to watching others being hurt formed and drove her to willingly sacrifice herself to help.

At what point does Willa's coerced compliance transition to being an accomplice?

Another splash of garlic mixed with bile hit the back of her throat, burning it. *Gads, the soup had been a bad idea.* Willa was a complication. One Phe needed to figure out how to deal with immediately.

Phe wrapped her hand around her amulet. The three braids on either side of the suspended drop of water pressed into her palm. Its presence grounded her, reminded her she could do anything.

The tread of shoes snapped Phe's gaze to the open doorway. Her heart stood at attention—not knowing if it should run or freeze.

"Lady Orphne." The General's gaze drilled into Phe's as he closed the distance between them, with Willa slowing trailing him. He'd changed out of his black suit and into a casual burnt orange sweater vest with slacks.

Phe's grip on her amulet tightened, and tinges of pain burst where the bracelet disturbed the wound.

She immediately recognized the General now that the mask was gone. His short brown hair was styled with some sort of product that made his hair glisten. He carried the same features as his family, though edgier—which gave him a dark look. He had a round face, high cheekbones, a defined nose, and dimples that flashed when he smiled. Like they were right then.

Seskel Brevil.

She held her breath as he circled her, his fingertips leaving burning trails across her as they traced along her as one would trail a finger along a dresser or the wall. He stopped behind her, wrapped a hand around her waist, and pulled her flush against his body.

The thick petticoats muffled the contact of his legs, only so far, because he was taller than her. Hating the contact, Phe's shoulders sprung to her ears, and her spine curved, which didn't deter him. A possessive hand splayed across her stomach, while his other pressed against her collarbones, straightening her, fingers resting ominously close to her neck.

An eruption of burning agony stabbed into Phe's flesh at every point of contact.

He inhaled deeply then growled, "Orphne, welcome home," her hair moving with his words. "She smells amazing," he stated, and the way Willa tensed had Phe assuming he'd locked gazes with her.

"Sir, I didn't remove her amulet," Willa confessed. "But I thoroughly cleaned it."

Seskel released Phe, only to step in front of her and clasp her chin —forcing her to meet his gaze. His fingernails threatened to leave crescent shaped cuts on her jawbone.

Phe blinked, trying to clear the rush of fresh pain hitting her behind her eyes.

"It's rumored Her Grace created it as a symbol of their friendship, and she wears it all the time. She can keep it on for now."

Kyra had made the bracelet for Phe after the Drykz Forest incident. The amulet was a constant reminder of Kyra and sea sistership. Their friendship had formed eight years ago—Phe had been ten and Kyra eleven—when Grum had attempted to use Phe to kidnap Kyra. Somehow, their friendship had withstood the battering of Phe's past as well as their vastly different personalities and circumstances.

"You did an exceptional job cleaning her up. She looks and smells perfect." Then he addressed Phe, "Do you feel better, Orphne?"

Phe subtly bobbed her chin yes.

It wouldn't bode well for her if she told Seskel the truth. She'd roll in General Bastion's sewage pile a million times over if it meant the General wouldn't touch her. Plus, Phe rarely spoke—another remnant from Grum.

With a shallow, shaky breath, she refocused. *What do I know about him?*

Seskel was the third son of a prominent and well-liked Parliament official, Zankel Brevil, and seven years her senior, making him twenty-five. The senior Mr. Brevil was one of Kyra's favorite politicians because of his linear focus on many of the societal issues Kyra advocated for. Kyra included him and his family on her list of invitees for events, both large and intimate. Seskel always attended.

Seskel had two brothers, Zaster and Cithias. Zaster was following in his father's footsteps, and his grandfather's before him. Cithias was leading the family business of importing and exporting a variety of products.

Seskel, the third and last child of Zankel, was a self-proclaimed entrepreneur but seemed to struggle with finding his place. He'd started two separate companies that fell apart. Rumors had swirled through society, whispering that Seskel's business practices were not up to the same standards as his family's. Even though the rumors had been immediately stopped, no one else partnered with him, leaving his days free to help Cithias with the family business, and his nights free to host parties. Seskel was known for his parties.

Seskel was also the only member of the Brevil family that hadn't completed his time in the Xafarian military. *Why hadn't he?*

Phe ruffled through memory after memory, trying to dredge up anything that could help trigger any recall, yet when it came to the hush-hush rumors of his discharge from the military, there was nothing. A gaping black hole. She bit the inside of her cheek hard, trying to clear her mind of the cloud of panic and pain. This was not the time for mistakes.

"Leave us," Seskel said to Willa. "I will call for you when I'm done."

At his command, shivers scurried down Phe's body. Sweat beaded at her hair line and armpits. Her limbs became weighted, useless appendages. Lady Orphne's rising tide of panic flooded her.

The snick of the wood door closing catapulted Phe's heart rate.

What else do you know about Seskel? she coached, fighting the current of emotions. If she could keep her brain thinking beyond her terror, beyond her Lady Orphne persona, maybe it wouldn't drown her. *The Brevils?*

Seskel was inches from her face, his dark gaze peering through her, as if he was trying to delve into her soul and expose all her secrets.

Phe blinked, shuttering her gaze and wrapping those secrets tightly to her. She lived in a precarious, mirrored house, and nobody had full access. Not even Kyra.

Kyra.

Dredging up Kyra's name was the lifeboat Phe needed to wrangle her panic and recenter, because Phe had dedicated her life to being the best warrior, the best assassin, to be Kyra's ultimate secret weapon. Even though this mission had nothing to do with protecting Kyra, invoking her name settled her. *What else do I know about the Brevils?*

The Brevils had multiple properties throughout Oceanid: three mansions, a country house, and several apartments in the seaport district.

The most logical conclusion was that she was at their countryside manner, not just because of the rolling fields she'd glimpsed through the carriage curtains—it was more basic than that. Seskel lived in his family's countryside estate, and it was the perfect location to set up headquarters for a clandestine operation.

"*Lady* Orphne." Seskel's grip loosened, and he circled his thumb in a light pain-smearing caress on her cheek. "I have been waiting a long time for this moment and, to be honest, had never expected it to come to fruition." Seskel drew her face forward, so close his woodsy, bourbon-coated breath warmed her cheeks, coating them in a layer of moisture.

How long had he been waiting? The hair on her nape stood on end.

"Yet here you are, finally." It was impressive how Seskel infused delight and menace into his words. He hauled her into his body, again, this time eviscerating any air separating their lower halves.

Phe strained away from him, her entire being screaming with agonizing discomfort. *Please stop touching me.* All thoughts of the Brevils, their properties, what she knew about Seskel, and where she was, vanished. *Please stop touching me.* A vice seized her throat, siphoning her air supply to a trickle. *Please stop touching me.*

Seskel tightened his grip, effortlessly eradicating the small space she'd created. Humor lines etched into the corners of his eyes. "Oh no, Orphne. The only space you'll be given is what I allow." Seskel angled her head to the side, exposing her neck, then gently ran his nose along her cheek. "We have so much to learn about each other."

A scalding hot lava stream of pain followed his movement, veining off into tributaries of searing pain that tunneled into her head.

Oh seas, don't touch my neck. Don't touch my neck. Oh seas, don't touch my neck, she beseeched, petrified he'd trigger one of her body's visceral memories of Grum strangling her. *I can't have a flash. Not now.*

Her breath came in short, fast bursts and all the blood in her head plummeted to her feet. *He's not Grum.* She tried to convince her body, but her body was having none of it. Her vision blurred at the edges.

When he released her, she sprang backwards like a loaded spring, only to be stopped by his grip on her arms.

"You're deliciously reactive." Seskel examined her with a half-smile—one Phe'd seen him use over the years at social functions. Seskel's twinkling gaze leisurely traveled the length of her body, coating her in a layer of slime. "Now, on to the rules."

Slight tremors raked Phe from the inside out. Her heart and chest shook with its force. *This was the worst. Idea. Ever.*

Seskel continued, gaze intensifying. "Willa will care for you daily. You *will* comply. Don't try to convince her to help you escape or to contact anyone. She's aware that if there are even rumors of you being here, her family will die, her friends will die, and she will die."

Phe'd already assessed Willa's position—it in no way, shape, or form included helping her.

"Rule one, you will address me as General and *verbally* respond to me." He flashed her a set of dimples, and his features softened. "I'm not completely heartless. I'll give you some leeway for a few days because I know speaking isn't natural for you. But you will speak to me when spoken to."

His eyes hardened for just a moment, and Phe's stomach dropped, her thoughts again going to Grum. Seskel brought her back to the moment, saying, "In the meantime, I'll think of a creative incentive to help you."

Phe bit into the flesh of her inner cheek, again, the movement tugging at the cuts on her mouth, reminding her of their presence. Grum had tried to make her talk in the beginning, too. Dread raced through her, she had a feeling their versions of incentives were drastically different—and Seskel's brand would trump Grum's.

She'd outlasted Grum—not by will, but by pure terror, until he found value in her silence. Seskel was not Grum, and she was not a powerless, voiceless child anymore. She was eighteen years old, and from the last eight years of General Bastion's brutal training, she had learned to pick her battles. Speaking did not need to make it onto this battlefield.

"Rule two, you will eat, drink, and take care of yourself. Three, you will not harm yourself."

Phe inwardly grunted. If she'd followed those rules in her own life, she wouldn't be here, worrying about what Seskel had planned for her or fighting her body's response to memories she'd long ago buried in a dark corner of her mind or being worried that this mission would break her.

She could almost hear Elzac's deep sigh, the one that conveyed he'd be simultaneously pleased with her realization and displeased with her choice.

In this situation, he'd definitely question Phe's decision. He'd ponder thoughtfully, his wise gaze steady, if she had a savior complex or if this was a subconscious drive to punish herself. Why else would she ever think putting herself in this position was a good idea?

It's both and then some. But now was not the time to dredge into her past and find the root reasons for her choices. No. She needed to survive this moment and the next and hope to the stars that Seskel— this mission—wasn't her fracturing point.

It wasn't as though there were other options.

"Rule four, you are never to leave these rooms unless it's with *me*." An involuntary shiver shot through her at the ice in his voice. "Rule five, no other men touch you—unless I give permission. Those are the ground rules we will start with today; do you understand?"

Phe quickly nodded her understanding, hoping she would not be there long enough for him give others permission to touch her.

Seskel's gaze sharpened, the skin of his face tightened.

Seas, right. She cleared her throat, swallowed once. Opened her mouth. Froze when she noticed Seskel's gaze had fixated there. Closed it, tight. Swallowed again.

"Orphne." Warning bleached her name, and Seskel's grip on her arms toughened.

Why was forcing these words out so hard?

With mammoth effort, lips practically sealed together, she mumbled, "Yes, General."

Head bowed, as if the effort of giving those two words had defeated her, she toyed with one of the three corded braids on her amulet. Her calloused fingertips followed the braid until she reached the middle of the bracelet, where a drop of water hovered unnaturally in the center. She stuck her finger into the water, a habit she'd picked up from Kyra, who consistently had a body part in water because it soothed her. It didn't soothe Phe.

"If you break these rules, I will punish you." A grim giddiness blossomed in his gaze, and his grip on her biceps tightened, as if this excited him.

Phe worked to swallow a lump in her throat—unsuccessfully.

Seskel's stony tone lightened, and a half smirk dimpled his cheek. He slid his hands down her arms, pried her hand away from her amulet, and interlaced their fingers. "I have a current guest in residence you need to meet." As soon as the words were out of his mouth, he tugged her toward the door from which he'd entered.

Phe's teeth sliced into her cheek until she tasted the coopery tang of her blood, which only briefly deflected the scorching pain of his hand on hers.

Seskel led her through the door, through his private ensuite dining area, and into a cozy library. Ignoring the only other door in the library, he brought her to the wall opposite the windows, notching his finger on top of the spine of a book called *Forbidden Pleasures.*

He paused and turned to her. "This is my playroom." Seskel twisted to face her. "Or shall I say, our playroom?" Then he tilted the book diagonally, and the wall became a door.

The lub-dub of Phe's heart went off kilter.

Seskel walked them into the room and into an oppressive cloud of fear and horror.

The room was windowless and illuminated with dim lighting. A girl was on the bed in the middle of the room, her arms and legs strapped to each bedpost. Messy dull brown hair peeked out of a muted black sheet that covered her from her shoulders to mid-thigh, exposing her pale limbs.

The girl's skin was a canvas of bruises and markings.

Phe's stomach heaved, and chunky fragments of that blasted stew filled her mouth. *Worst. Idea. Ever.* Swallowing the bile, she scanned the girl's prone form, watching breathlessly until she saw the rise and fall of the girl's chest.

Oh, thank the seas.

Phe tore her gaze away from the girl and took in the room. One wall was studded with rings hung at different heights, all of them featuring dangling handcuffs. Next to that were several racks that held paddles, whips, and an assortment of crops in a variety of sizes. Her eyes fell on the table with knives and clamps, but it was the cage —large enough to fit a person—on the floor that knocked the air from her as if she'd been punched in the gut.

Gads. A cage.

A cold sweat spouted at her neck, brow, and armpits. *Don't think about it.* Her gaze flew to the girl on the bed as she pummeled the wave of doom and horror that rose. She must have slowed her pace, or maybe Seskel heard her quick intake of breath, because he turned to her.

His pupils were blown, and the glint in his eyes had somehow magnified. Yet he was expressionless. Eerily so. His gaze traveled the contours of her face, and when his eyes met hers, his lips broke formation—dipping deeply at their edges.

"I see I've frightened you." Seskel lowered his tone, and it came out intimate and gentle, and it made Phe want to break his kneecaps. "Think of my playroom as a place where we'll explore your levels of pleasure and pain, like I am with Oriana."

Phe flicked Oriana's sleeping shackled form a glance. *If I don't say how wrong this is, am I as bad as Willa?* Phe dragged her lower lip into her mouth, wetting it. When she'd been beaten and restrained and powerless, all she'd wanted was for one of the people who'd passed through to have said something. Tried, even if it was in useless words, to help her.

Seskel's focus shifted to her mouth. She prepared to force words past numb lips, pointing out that Oriana was not there willingly. And that he was a monster.

While her tongue was forming the courage, she realized Lady Orphne—the timid, sickly, almost mute Lady Orphne—wouldn't say a thing. She pressed her lips together.

Seskel hummed, concern wrinkling the corners of his eyes. "You bring up a good point."

Phe blinked, confused. *What?*

"I can't treat you like the others." Seskel tucked a strand of hair behind Phe's ear. "You're special. You've always been special and fragile and sickly and submissive." He leaned into her, his warm dry lips brushing her ear. "Deliciously submissive." The pleasure that wrapped around his words made her want to wretch, and she forced the garlicky bile back down. "If I were to treat you like your imposters, you wouldn't last. Not with your disposition—and we're going to live long lives together." Seskel lifted their intertwined hands to his mouth and kissed her knuckles.

All Phe could do was stare unblinkingly at him.

"I will continue to host . . ." Seskel tugged her forward, walking backwards to the bed. Phe darted a peek at Oriana. The girl hadn't moved, yet her body was no longer lax with sleep. Wide eyes— showing more white than pupils—watched them. ". . . girls like Oriana, because I have peculiar tastes and needs."

Seskel's legs bumped into the bed, and he gracefully perched on its edge. The look in his eyes changed; the gaze he locked onto Oriana was pure, uncensored darkness.

Seskel released their intertwined fingers, and slowly wrapped his hand around Oriana's nape, his thumb softly circling her jaw like he'd done to Phe. "Do you see her resemblance to you, Orphne?" Seskel tore his gaze from Oriana's, capturing Phe's. "Even her name is slightly similar."

Phe wet her dry lips, the cut corners stinging as her tongue hit them. What she saw was a young woman who'd been stripped, tortured, and had the misfortune of having the same dull brown hair color as Phe. Phe dragged in a breath, hating herself for going along with General Bastion's plan. Hating that she hadn't considered going rogue and hunting every single one of these people down on her own —dishing out her own justice. But that was exactly why she hadn't. Acting as judge and jury and executioner would skirt too closely to becoming Grum.

Finally, after a stretch of silence broken only by Oriana's breathing, Phe whispered, "Yes, General."

Seskel stood, his whole body taut. They were so close, Phe could feel tension radiating off him—or was it excitement? The glimmer returned to his gaze, and, with his pointer finger, he lifted her chin to meet his inspection. "Good girl."

Phe dug her nails into her ribcage. Blinking rapidly, she hoped he couldn't read in her eyes how wrong he was.

Seskel traced Phe's jaw, his gaze tracking his movement. "Your skin is so soft," he muttered, transfixed.

The rustling of sheets snapped Seskel's attention onto Oriana. His perverse gaze caressed her shackled form. Seskel stalked to one of the racks, fingers sweeping across the selection of whips as if he was casually choosing a shirt to wear for the day. "Oriana here was a bad girl. She tried to escape."

Oriana shook so much the sheet slipped further off her, revealing the spectrum of colors and cuts on her exposed torso.

Seskel chose one, returning with a bullwhip in hand. "Orphne, this is what happens when someone tries to escape. Stand back."

Paralyzed, Phe watched as Oriana stared, unseeing, past Phe's shoulder. Phe's gaze shot back to Seskel as he shook the whip free and flicked it.

Without thinking, Phe threw herself across Oriana as the whip sizzled through the air. Both girls grunted, and a lashing pain slashed a line across her mid-back. Phe hissed and curled around Oriana protectively.

"No!!" Seskel roared, hurling himself onto the bed. He ripped her off Oriana and towed her all the way into the golden suite. There was a wildness to his gaze, and his palms skimmed across the fabric of her dress. "Are you hurt?"

If the whip had hit Oriana, it could've split her wide open. Instead, it hit Phe's corseted back. A raw tingle marked the path of the whip, and her dress pinched tightly. She couldn't lie; if he made her undress now, or tomorrow, she wouldn't be able to hide the welt. "Yes, General."

"Rule." He had a bruising grip on her biceps. "Three." He twisted her and worked his finger in between her skin and corset, checking for blood. When he seemed satisfied she wasn't bleeding, he grabbed her with both hands, fingers on her neck.

The edges of her vision tunneled until all she could see were Seskel's eyes. Flecks of gold and black swirled in them, and she had the odd thought they were strikingly beautiful. If only they didn't belong to this depraved man.

"You were not supposed to do that," Seskel growled, pushing her. She stumbled. Seskel pointed at her. "Rule six, no interfering with my guests. You're too delicate." Then he strode to another door, yanked it open, and called into the hallway. "You and you, in here."

Phe crossed her arms, hugging herself. Lady Orphne would never have done that. Lady Orphne was more likely to cower behind Seskel, ears covered, than throw herself in the fray. *I'm failing.*

Then there was her tunneled vision. *What if I'd had a flash?*

"Now I have to punish you." His jaw set in a grim line, as if he had been served cold injustice. He addressed the two henchmen who entered the room. "She'll sleep with the monster tonight. Make sure it's chained. You're to guard her and make sure she's not hurt. And remember, she's mine."

The burly henchmen converged on her, only to pause at Seskel's harsh voice. "Orphne, I can just as easily throw you out with the trash as I can treat you like my queen. I hope you spend tonight considering this, because the next set of punishments won't be so innocuous." Then to the men, he said, "Get her out of here."

The door clicked shut behind her as the henchmen corralled her out, but not before she heard Seskel mutter, "Now, Oriana. Where were we?"

The words alone caused icy dread to trail down her spine, but it was his tone, full of anticipation and darkness, that truly terrified her.

What have I done?

5

The moment she was out of Seskel's grasp, her panic faded to a slight undercurrent. Spending a night near a chained monster—when Seskel only wanted to instill the fear of the seas in her—was like sending her on holiday.

"Got dealt a bad hand tonight," the bigger of the two henchmen said. He was only a few inches taller than Phe but made up for it by pure bulk. His shirt stretched tightly—probably because it wasn't designed for a man of his mass—across slabs of muscle. His face featured bushy eyebrows that seemed to melt into his beard. If Kyra saw this man, she would swoon with excitement and proclaim him a werewolf by sight alone. He was a wolf of a man.

The other man, who was taller and with a small port belly, rolled his neck in tense agreement. A plume of stale smoke hovered like a nasty haze on his clothing. She'd name him Ferment because of it. Ferment slowed his gait. His thick, calloused fingers clenched her right bicep, digging the fabric of the sleeve into her. A deep ache pulsed under his fingers, his touch less distressing because of the barrier of her dress but still painful.

"I heard once it has your scent, you're done," Ferment said.

"She's the one who should worry. Not us. We're not sleeping with it." The lantern Wolf man carried hung from his massive paw, barely illuminating the path.

They passed the last outbuilding and a huge stable. The dirt path ended, yet they didn't stop. Fencing lined the area to her right. To her left was a clear field until a line of trees broke its horizon. That's where they were headed—well past the sight of the house.

Phe wondered if where they were taking her was where they held the rest of the hostages. Maybe this monster was one way for them to control them?

Wolf man shrugged, uneasy. "I don't buy into all that yammering. As far as I've heard, there's been no proof. At least we're not sleeping with it." He kicked a rock in the path, sending it tumbling into a bush. "Lady, do you know what the monster is?"

"Like she would," Ferment scoffed, his voice strained. "Tell her."

"It's a creature from Drykz Forest," Wolf man said as fast as he could get the words out. As if the act of naming the forest would call its attention.

Phe glanced between the two. It couldn't be. Drykz Forest's creatures never ventured out of its perimeter, and if they had, the whole of Xafara would be up in arms about it because those things were true monsters that wouldn't stop killing until they were dead. Yet both men had tight shoulders and matching expressions.

A trepidatious zing zipped up her spine.

"Yeah, I heard a farmer found it wandering in one of his fields, alone. Thought something must have happened to its mother. He took in it and, BAM!" Wolf man clapped his hands loudly. "Next day all his livestock was dead and the monster was covered in their blood."

"I heard the whole family died, too. Ripped the family apart, limb by limb, and gnawed on their bones." Ferment's voice dropped to a conspiratorial whisper. "Their neighbors discovered the whole mess and trapped the monster. One of their sons—who works here—came to work and couldn't stop talking about it. Poor lad was so scared. Word soon got to the master and piqued his interest, and now it's here."

The line of trees broke ahead, and a dilapidated frame came into view. Even in the low light, Phe could make out the skeleton of a fence encircling a paddock area at the back of the shed.

"It won't die," Wolf man tacked on. "They've tried to kill it. Beat it to death. Starved it. Even tried to take its head once . . . We lost a head or two that day, but not the monster's."

The musty scent of mold mingled with urine and feces and decay. The wood to the outer wall was cracked and sagging in places. Patches of green lichen grew on its sides. In comparison, the door they stopped at was brand new. Its timber shone with the rawness of its recent felling. The handle and lock that Wolf man fumbled to open one handedly—was strong, thick metal with the crisp lines of newness.

Wolf man pulled the door open, its metal hinges screaming, and the wood dragged roughly against the dirt ground. He lifted the lantern to face level—blinding Phe and leaving floating orbs of light in her vision—and peered in.

"It's chained," Wolf man announced, stepping back.

Ferment crowded her into the opening. "We need to secure her."

"Yeah, yeah we should." Wolf man thrust his lantern into the darkened opening, then jumped at the rolling rumble that emitted from the darkened room. With his free hand, Wolf man searched the wall until he found a handful of metal chains, pulling them toward her with a rattling clang.

"What do you think? All of 'em?"

"Yes, in case we're called away." Ferment nodded, emphasizing the end of the sentence.

Wolf man grunted and set to work strapping the restraints on her wrist, ankles, and waist.

"You won't be going anywhere, miss," Wolf man said, double-checking his work.

"Nor will she be in danger of throwing herself at the monster either," Ferment added. "You know, in case she had any ideas to end it all."

A hard push hurled her into the decrepit stable, and she tripped as the chains stopped her, landing in a pile of manure. The noxious smell of the dung she'd landed in, combined with ammonia and mildew, hit her like a punch to the face. Her eyes instantly watered, and her throat burned, as she scrambled back toward the door.

"Sleep well, lass," one of the two men called, his voice obscured by the slamming of the door but not enough to hide the edge of laughter in it. "We'll see you in the morning."

It was darker in here, and the remnants of the lantern flame blurred her vision with orbs. She squinted, trying to distinguish what was in there with her. The clang of metal locking into place pierced through the buzzing of a swarm of flies.

Instinctively, she imagined wrapping the room's shadows around her in an invisible cloak. This was something she'd done since she could remember, bundling herself in darkness and wishing for invisibility. It was a residue from her time with Grum—when not being seen meant not being hurt.

A low rumble-shriek filled the silence, followed by the clinking of metal chains and the scraping sound of something pawing at the ground.

Heart galloping fiercely in her chest, Phe spun toward the noise and shuffled in the opposite direction until she was against the wall, willing her eyes to adjust to the darkness faster. The ground was uneven and clumpy, and what she assumed was hay pricked her ankles. The rough wood of the wall scratched at the fine threads of her dress, no doubt pulling them. Pressing against the wall zinged her still stinging whip lash.

Her heart steadied into a uniform rhythm. If a monster had actually broken the boundary of Drykz Forest, General Bastion would throw all his viable forces into killing it.

A glimmer of red flared in the right corner, sending her heart sprinting.

The chains rattled.

A visceral terror grasped the lobes of her lungs. All the fine hairs on her body stood up.

In the months she'd been trapped in the haunted—or cursed—

Drykz Forest, Phe had seen some of the fiercest, most bloodthirsty monsters. And one of the fiercest had had a sheen of red to its eyes.

It can't be.

If it were a Drykz Forest monster, it would be attacking and screeching and attracting even more of its brethren. Because that's what they did. Stumble on one and the next moment, you had a horde of them intent on rending you to shreds.

I'm not in the forest. Rational thought punched through her seizing frontal lobe. *And Seskel doesn't want to hurt me.* He wanted her to know what it felt like to be treated as though she was worthless—seas, was he late for that party—and to be scared, alone, cold. He wanted obedience.

He wanted her submission.

Her total submission. Having her mauled by an animal wasn't in his plans. He wanted to do all the mauling. Her lungs ached as they drew in a long, calming breath. *Gads, this place needs to be burned to the ground.* Maybe she would, after this investigation was wrapped up. For now, prying open the paddock door was the best she could do, and she could only hope those fools hadn't done a proper check of the shed.

The red glimmer disappeared.

Slowly, the floating orbs in her vision dissolved, and she could make out the outline of the paddock door and boarded up window.

The animal—because that's the only explanation for what this monster could be—moved out of the shadows. It was big. Its back easily reached Phe's ribcage. Its head extended toward her, ears flat, and around its neck . . . was that a horse's mane?

"You're a *horse*?" Her voiced sailed into the high octaves of bewilderment.

It did its weird grumble-growl-shriek.

"Shhh . . ." she whispered, ignoring the sense that the horse had responded to her. Tentatively, she stepped toward it, her chains rattling with the movement. "I won't hurt you."

It snorted and flipped its mane. Phe got the distinct impression that it said, "Yeah, right."

"I get that. I wouldn't trust me either," Phe acknowledged, peering intensely at it. "What have these vile people been doing to you?"

This time, it huff-whined.

"Bad things?" Phe was close enough now that she could finally make out more details. What she saw caused angry tremors to ripple through her like the prelude to an earthquake.

Maybe it was because Seskel no longer hovered menacingly, with his blistering touches and nefarious sexual intent. Maybe it was because now that she was alone, and her past no longer kept resurfacing like a bloated body, she could think of the others who'd been taken and tortured.

Maybe it was because of those things, and more, that she was now mad.

Raging, world-destroying livid.

The "monster" they'd found, in a field, without its mother, was a baby horse.

A foal.

It pranced a step, its ears lowering again, and this time it flashed its teeth.

That stopped her. *Does it have fangs?* No. Must be her eyes.

Phe inhaled deeply and held it for a count of four, then slowly released on the same count.

Inhale: *I am a sea of calm.*

Exhale: *my anger.*

Inhale: *I will avenge them.*

Exhale: *anger.*

She repeated this until her heart no longer sang of vengeance, her nails no longer dug into her palms, and her anger settled.

"I'm sorry," she cooed, skimming the foal's skeletal form.

Sharp ends of its ribs had splintered, protruding against its skin. Its front knees were double the size of Phe's fist, and its hide was a patchwork of whip lashes. Some were old, thick scabs, but there was a section on its back . . .

Phe wrenched her gaze away. Her own injury from Seskel's whip throbbed to the pounding rhythm of her heart. A sickening prickling skittered up her spine. Phe knew what it was like to have her skin rendered to pulp.

How is it standing?

All of Drykz Forest's creatures could withstand an immense level of injury. The thought sent a spark of fear. Then the foal's front legs buckled, and it collapsed to the ground in a soft thud. The whites of its eyes flashed—and relief flooded Phe. It must have held itself up by sheer will and adrenaline. It wasn't a creature from Drykz Forest.

There was something about the fierceness of this creature that struck Phe. An unwillingness to give up that she could relate to— even when the immediate future offered no relief.

"Oh, baby. I promise. I won't hurt you." Phe tested her manacles but couldn't slide her hands through. She might have had to come on this mission without the comfort of her weapons, but she didn't come without her pick.

Phe clasped her amulet, pinching the edge of the leather with her thumb and forefinger until she found her hidey hole. Digging the thin, sturdy pick out, she set to work on removing her own restraints.

She flicked a glance at the horse, for the first time grateful she was forced to act as—to be—her Lady Orphne version. Everyone would underestimate her.

Once she was free, she leaned against the door and closed her eyes, synching her breath as she dove into a deeper awareness. Eyes closed, she listened for Ferment and Wolf man, but they were long gone.

She reached awkwardly behind her, untying and then loosening her dress so she could slip out of it. Next, she discarded her petticoats. Goosebumps rose on her exposed flesh at the nippy temperature.

Phe set about arranging her clothing to appear as though she was off to the side, sleeping, just in case her guards returned to check on her. Then she slowly made her way to the paddock door with the weight of the foal's gaze on her. She ran her fingers over the wood, felt the rusty hinges.

She set about pulling the hinges off. The top one was easy, as the bolt had already half-wiggled itself free. The bottom one took some spit, the use of the other bolt to help pry and loosen it, muscle, and a few choice words before Phe could yank—with aching fingers—the bolt free. Then she lifted the door and cracked it open.

Fresh clean air tickled her senses and spun the straggling pieces of hair into her face. Stars glittered above her, welcoming her into the comfort of night. Reaching for her shadows, she imagined cloaking herself in their embrace, an embrace she'd need as she was clothed only in a white corset, matching lacy underwear, and muddied slippers.

Preparing to slip out, she glanced at the foal. It lay exactly as it had fallen. Tense. Tracking her. Its breaths caused the wreckage of its chest to waver. A rush of sadness clenched Phe's heart. She knew she should kill it. Put it out of its misery. Yet, beyond the fact she couldn't kill it tonight, she didn't want to. There was life and fight left in it. Who was she to decide its life should end because its injuries looked bleak? She knew from experience, if you set your mind on healing, anything was possible.

Slipping into the overgrown meadow, she decided—when she was done searching the property—she'd bring it food and water. Because, even if she couldn't rescue it, she had to do something to help it.

6

Phe's eyelids drooped, and her head wobbled, jerking her awake. After the henchman had returned her to Willa's care early that morning, she'd spent the entire day outside on the balcony, and now it was nearly dinnertime. She compelled herself to watch the descending dusk, grateful Seskel had yet to make an appearance, and relaxed into the ultra-plush, oversized armchair she sat on, overlooking a vast garden. A breeze fluttered the hair around her ears, bringing with it the scent of azaleas.

A scent Phe was quickly growing an aversion to.

A canvas stand loomed on her right with an array of paints laid out to the side of it, like a set of interrogation tools. She'd sketched the garden halfheartedly and used the muted, dull colors they'd given her to speckle the canvas. But she couldn't bring herself to do more. Even the flat colors were too bright for this evil place.

Last night, she'd slipped into all the outbuildings she'd passed, searching for something, anything that could possibly help her figure out if Seskel was holding more captives on the premises. There had been nothing.

She hadn't thought it'd be that easy, especially knowing that Seskel's playroom was a secret room off his private library. Yet last night wasn't a total waste. She'd found a sleeping drought in the main stable—probably for the stable hands.

She didn't want to play her hand too quickly, though. She needed to know if Willa and Seskel followed a routine. Once a pattern was established and their guard dropped, then she would use the drought on Willa.

Phe scanned the tree line until she found the familiar shape of a hawk she'd been watching all day. Its mere presence, for some reason, reassured her. It reminded her of Ihrone. He had an affinity toward animals, and she'd caught him interacting with them a few times over the years.

She wished she had Ihrone's ability. After lugging grain and water and some hay to the shed last night, the little foal had adamantly refused to accept it from her. A part of her understood. The foal had no reason to trust her. If their roles were reversed, she wouldn't. Heck, it'd been eight years since Grum and trusting was still an issue for her, among other things. What was the saying, you can lead a horse to water but can't force them to drink? So, she'd set about—moving slower than molasses—hiding the grain and water within the foal's reach.

Phe scrubbed her eyes, the movement straining the raw patches on her wrists. Sitting, all docile and sickly and weak, was killing her. It didn't matter that this was her strategic plan, patience was not a virtue she had. She was not even friends with patience—they fought, often.

She wanted to continue scouring the grounds for anyone hidden on the property. She wanted to check on the foal and make sure no spineless, nasty person was hurting her again. She wanted to check on Oriana. Apologize to her for sharing the same shade of hair and eyes. She wanted to send a missive to General Bastion, tell him Seskel Brevil was the General and tell him the Brevils' countryside estate housed at least one sex trafficking victim.

She couldn't do any of those things, because Willa—the guard dog—sat in the golden room glaring daggers into the back of her head all day.

It didn't help that her fear ground on her like two tectonic plates vying for position. Soon, Seskel would emerge. Even though she kept bringing her brain back to the mission, back to her warrior Phe, just as quickly, it would return to him. Him and his roaming hands and sniffy nose. Him and her Lady Orphne persona. Him and his resemblance to Grum. And as much as she tried—and she tried—the echoes of Grum slithered into her mind and heart, screaming at her.

Who knew what torturous plans he had?

A soft tread approached, this time from the adjoining room, and her heart stuttered. *It's him.* She couldn't help the anxiety that cramped her stomach, rolling and twisting it in ways that if she'd had food or water in it, would have had her in the bathroom. As it was, she took deep breaths to keep the bile in place, then burrowed into the chair, bit her inner cheek, clutched her amulet, and fixed her gaze on the door handle.

It moved.

Phe's breath faltered.

Willa straightened to the height of the pole she seemed to have jammed inside her. The door opened, revealing Seskel.

Phe's heart fainted dead, face-planting into her lungs.

Seskel's gaze captured hers immediately, and a smile dimpled his cheeks. Unlike her, he appeared refreshed and well rested, glowing with a vibrancy Phe couldn't name.

"Leave us," he commanded Willa, who immediately vanished.

Her melodramatic heart clawed itself to its feet and thu-thunked hard, restarting.

She anxiously rolled a braid on her amulet between her fingers. Swallowing several times, she tried to control her body's engrained reaction, but she only managed to make herself more of a vibrating beacon of fear.

In a last-ditch effort, like a drowning man clinging to a piece of driftwood, she funneled all her thoughts and envisioned Oriana. Strapped to that bed, her limbs extended by those straps, the mass of dull brown hair and similarly colored eyes. The bruises. The whip.

Her heart took the memory and erected a wall around itself. It still quivered and rocked, but something in it solidified. It knew she was here for the girls and boys like Oriana—but it didn't mean it wasn't scared out of its ever-loving mind because Lady Orphne was at the helm.

"Good evening, Orphne." Seskel's shadow blanketed her, sending a chill through her. He stopped to examine her aborted painting, peering at the garden and comparing her work to nature's masterpiece. Her sketch was dismal in comparison.

Phe stared at his calves, her mouth bone dry. Her fingertips tingled, and a cold sweat sprouted on her nape. She hated that her body reacted this way. Hated that the remnants of Grum boiled to the surface in Seskel's presence. Hated that her Lady Orphne persona embodied everything weak, sick, and fearful. Hated that she couldn't be warrior Phe.

He switched his raptorial gaze to her and leaned in, placing both hands on either side of her head, all traces of his smile gone. "This is when you say, 'Good evening, General.'"

Phe opened her mouth—no sound came out. She closed it and nervously wet her lips.

Seskel's gaze dropped to her mouth, then to her throat.

Swallowing multiple times, she finally croak-mumbled, "Good evening, General."

"How was your night?" His focus shifted to the slightly bruised skin under her eyes from lack of sleep.

Phe inhaled her grunt—her normal response—and forced out, "Scary, General."

Seskel brought one hand to cup her chin, and slowly—watching Phe's reaction—dragged the other over her dress to her breast. "I have been waiting so long for this." He squeezed.

Black pinpricks dotted her visions. She couldn't breathe, no matter how hard she sucked air in. Her head became fuzzy. Distally, she heard the hawk screech, and she commiserated with it, because she was screaming on the inside, too.

Seskel nuzzled the side of her face, neck. His fingers pulled at the fabric of her bodice, working to expose her chest and corset.

One second, she was looking at Seskel's dark hair, the next Grum's hate-filled eyes and sandy blond hair filled her vision. The flash was disorienting. Grum had never touched her like this. Yes, he had been violent, but he had never crossed that line to sexual.

Seskel's tongue trailed her jawline, bringing her back to the present. She could feel new bruises forming under his fingers where he gripped her. "I am going to show you how pain can be pleasurable," he murmured silkily against her skin. "And when I'm done with you, you'll be begging me for more."

Oh seas! Oh seas! Oh seas! Phe squeezed her eyes shut and tried to push away—but there was no room.

Suddenly, Seskel stiffened and shifted, and those gold-and-black-flecked eyes of his collided with hers. His hand on her chest froze, and his warm breath splayed across her cheeks.

"This isn't right." His words skittered along her cheekbones. He licked his bottom lip, then sucked it in as he thought. "We can't do this." As if Phe was a consensual partner.

A shudder coursed through Phe.

Seskel tore himself away and strode to a wall, planting both of his hands flat and leaning into them. His head hung, and it looked like he was taking big gulping breaths.

Every molecule in Phe was still, fixated on the monster in the room.

Time passed, it could have been a minute or five, before Seskel straightened and returned to crouch in front of her. "I've wanted you since the moment I first set eyes on you, eight years ago." Seskel's gaze bore into hers. "It was right when you'd started living at House Nereid, after the botched attempt on Her Grace's life. My parents dragged me with them to check on Kyra and then set about immediately ignoring my presence. So, I snuck around the palace and came upon you. Do you remember?"

Phe shook her head, no. Those days were blurry. Grum had injured her, badly, and whenever she'd fall asleep, she'd be plunged into terrible nightmares or she'd lose time, lost in the ethers of her mind, or experience one of her flashes. It'd been bad. Then there was

General Bastion—who immediately began his regime of poisons on her.

Seskel gave her a salty half smile. "I'd noticed a servant leaving a room carrying bloodied bandages, and that quirked my interest. They'd left the door ajar, so I peeked in and there you were, in a corner on the floor. Blood was splattered all around you. Your eyes were so wide, so scared, and yet so defiant. You were struggling with a woman, and it took me a moment to realize, but she was trying to restrain you from hurting yourself.

"I must have made a noise, because instantly your gaze captured mine. You slipped from the woman's grasp, eyes still on me, and jabbed your hand into an open gash on your thigh. Your whole body relaxed from it. You craved the pain. You needed the pain. I knew in that instant, you were it for me.

"The woman yanked your hand away, forcing you to look at her again, and you bared your teeth at her. Then your face screamed, yet no noise came out of your mouth. I almost went in there, ripped the woman from you, and took you to be mine right then and there—but the servant returned and shooed me."

Oh stars. The woman must have been Jallia, who'd relentlessly stayed by her side, night and day, making sure she didn't hurt herself. Caring for her the best anyone could when stuck with a feral, traumatized, sleep-deprived child. The only time Phe would settle was when Kyra was with her, which Phe assumed had something to do with their special bond.

Seskel peered at her bodice. He moved deliberately, bringing his hand to it and smoothing the fabric he'd mussed into place.

"I wanted to take you so many times over the years. *So many times.* But I wasn't ready, and you." Seskel rested his hand on her thigh. "You closed everyone out, as if you were waiting for me."

His lips dipped into a frown. "My tastes have evolved since then too, and I'm used to taking what I want, when I want. But with you . . . I want more than what I can take. I want *all* of you. I want your heart, your devotion, your submission, all your pain and pleasure, and I daresay, I want to fill your belly with my children." He massaged her thigh, and his gaze followed his movements.

Phe's heart raced as he inched his hand toward her.

He pushed away from her, shoved his hands into pockets, making the tent in his pants even more noticeable, and paced a few steps away. He stopped, one hand left his pocket to run over his neatly styled hair, mussing it, then he pinned her with his gaze. "We'll take this slow. Real slow."

The shudder turned into tremors.

Seskel's shoulders tensed, and his fist knocked against his thigh, as if he was getting blood to it. "And I will woo you because you are the one for me."

With that, he strode across the room and into his, quietly closing the door behind him.

Crusty seas and flipping stars. This man had been obsessed with her for eight years. Eight years. Thoughts scrambled through her mind. He wanted to have babies with her. He'd seen her in *that* state. The state that was currently working its way from her core like an erupting volcano. Uncontrollable. The residue of his touches, of his initial intent, bathing her.

Phe curled into herself, unable to stop shaking.

7

"Phe." The single syllable battered through Phe's nervous system. Tension flared throughout her body and yanked her attention to the darkened balcony.

A shadow moved to her left.

"Roar?" Phe whispered, swiveling to search for Willa. "What are you doing? You can't be here. I have a babysitter; she could return any moment."

Roar crouched in front of her, dressed in black from the hat covering his muted auburn hair to his shoes. "Don't worry about your servant. She's preoccupied for the moment. I'm here to extract you."

"Don't tell me to not worry." Phe slit her eyes. Like that was possible. This mission had been a maelstrom of emotions from the moment she agreed to it. "And what do you mean, extract?"

Phe unlocked her interlaced fingers from around her legs and stiffly lowered her feet to the ground. She clenched and unclenched her fists, coaxing blood into them. "My mission just started."

They think I've failed already.

"We've reconsidered the plan and decided it would be best to pull you." Roar's steady blue gaze traveled the contours of her face, then body, cataloguing her visible injuries and her torn dress.

"I'm fine," Phe whispered, not sounding convincing, but she couldn't go. She just got here. She compressed her mouth into a firm line, letting Roar read the determination in her expression.

One side of Roar's mouth lifted, but there was no humor to the movement. He let her lie fade into the gap between them. Roar was the commander of Shadow Unit, the elite military team General Bastion had assigned her to train and work with, and he knew her. Or at least he knew the portions of her she allowed him to, and he wasn't buying her "I'm fine" statement.

"You can't pull me. I just got here." Phe sat taller. Lives depended on her. She realigned the torn fabric of her bodice, combing her mind. The last thing she remembered was Seskel closing the door to his suite. That had been at dusk. It was now dark, and obvious that time had passed. "I haven't discovered who the Colonel or the other captains are."

"You've helped identify the General," Roar explained, as if that was the objective of her mission when it wasn't. "It will only be a matter of time before we ID the others now."

Phe dropped her hands to her knees, gripping them. She couldn't leave now. What Seskel had done to her was nothing compared to what he was doing to Oriana. A shower of shame bathed Phe, causing a cold sweat to coat her. All Seskel had done was touch her, mostly over her clothing, and then he—bizarrely—vowed to woo her. Who knew what that meant?

Phe glanced at Seskel's door. "He has a secret room, and he's torturing Oriana, a girl, in there. If you want to extract anyone, take her." Crow's feet of tension webbed the corners of his eyes, his silent answer her suggestion.

"We're much closer to stopping this than we were yesterday," Roar countered, his face schooled to neutral.

"Not really." Phe shook her head, befuddled. Then, she lifted a brow. "Unless you were able to identify the Colonel and captains in the last twenty-four hours? Or were you able to find out where they are holding people?"

"We're adjusting the plan because we're unwilling to risk you."

Roar's tone was diplomatic.

They didn't think she could do it. Tingles of alarm rippled through her. Was her incompetence so blatant that they had to remove her immediately? What about the people who couldn't escape? She couldn't leave them.

"Last night I checked all the outbuildings, and now that you're here, I assume General Bastion had them checked, too. Tonight, I plan to..." The rest of Phe's sentence fell with Roar's shaking head.

"But why?" she whispered. She hadn't called for help. She'd been managing. Barely. But still, managing.

Roar's worry lines deepened. "We've had eyes on you since you arrived."

Phe flinched as if he'd hit her. She was notoriously private, and knowing they'd watched *that* ... Vitriol burned her taste buds.

"After witnessing what happened tonight and monitoring your reaction for the past few hours—"

"My reaction?" Her face scrunched with the question. How had she reacted? She'd been sitting right here.

"You've sat, unmoving, eyes distant for hours. You've been unresponsive to your servant during that time, not rousing after she touched you several times."

"Are you sure?" Phe hadn't had a space spell, where she detached from the present and drifted into her mental ethers completely unaware of her surroundings, for years.

"Yes."

Phe slumped into the chair, defeatedly sighing. How could she combat spacing and flashing and being touched? This entire mission was rigged for failure. She'd known it, on an intellectual level, going in. But now?

I've never failed.

I can't fail.

Not when there are other lives on the line.

Roar rocked to his feet, not bothering to offer her a hand, and strode toward the balcony's edge. "Come on, Phe."

Fighting every instinct to get up and walk away from this catastrophe in waiting, Phe sighed and anchored into the chair. "I'm not going."

"It's an order." Roar's tone never changed, but his shoulders tensed.

Phe rubbed her palms on her thighs and straightened her dress, avoiding his fiery gaze.

"You know the only person I accept orders from is Kyra. The rest of the time I take into consideration what is being asked, and I decide." Phe sucked in the courage to look at Roar, defiantly continuing.

"I've decided," she said pointedly, "that me staying is better for the operation than leaving. If I were to leave now, who knows how Seskel will react and how that will affect everything," leaving her real motivation unspoken.

Roar audibly sighed with understanding. "If you leave, it doesn't reflect badly on you. You haven't failed or acted incompetently. It's not your responsibility to save them."

Phe pinned him with her own fiery gaze. "That's not true. If I walk away with you now," she angrily whispered, feeling steam pour out of her nostrils, "I walk away from Oriana." She flung her arm toward the playroom. "And from the others taken with me, before me. To me, that's failure."

"It's self-preservation."

"What would I be preserving," Phe scoffed, "if I can't look at myself in the mirror?"

"Do you look at yourself in the mirror now?" He said it in his most neutral, calm voice, and yet it burrowed under her last nerve.

She narrowed her eyes and huffed.

Roar's tone softened, as did the lines of his face. "What if you're sacrificing too much?"

Phe's anger settled into embers in her chest. He was talking about her spacing episode. Her voice could cut trees. "I've recovered from my spacing before. I can do it again."

Roar returned to her side, squatting to just below eye level. This time, his face wasn't a reflection of a calm sea; worry for her had transformed his features. "What if it doesn't affect your spacing, but your ability to heal from your aversion to touch? What if it triggers your past and then you can't perform for Her Grace if needed?"

How in the seas did Roar manage to exude compassion when not a single muscle moved on his face?

"My abilities to protect Kyra have never been compromised by my past and never will be," she said harshly. Other than this situation, now—where she'd been ordered to maintain her Lady Orphne personality throughout the mission—she knew this to be true. There was no barrier that would hold her, whether it was people, environments, or her past. Not when it came to Kyra. With a degrading snort, she added. "And me? Be comfortable with touch?"

She waved a hand dismissively. "I realized long ago that wasn't in my future."

What was touch for any way? A sharing of a moment? Creating a deeper sense of connection in a relationship—like a mother to child, friends, or lovers? Beyond the scarred battleground of Grum, the reality was she lived a dual life.

When she was Lady Orphne, she used her aversion to touch to remind herself of who she was: sick, weak, timid. The festering discomfort of even the slightest contact kept her in her place.

How would she engage in a relationship with someone—not that she wanted to—if she was bound to only show them her Lady Orphne persona? She wasn't interested in the farce. Nor did she need it. Having survived the last eight years with minimal touch and a friend group, albeit very small, who understood this, she had no plans to change this. Not with the nasties in Oceanid.

Touch as Phe—the lethal weapon—was different. The touches, all under the auspices of combat training, made her come alive. Each touch fueled her and taught her lessons. It brought forth her power. Her skill. Her resiliency and determination. It made her Kyra's most deadly weapon.

Phe kept Roar's gaze, her severe tone and stony regard emphasized her nonnegotiable acceptance of this. "And I'm not worried about how it will trigger my past. It's nothing I haven't dealt with before."

"Phe, how old are you?" Compassion came from his blue eyes. They'd lost all intensity and were now soft pools of crystal blue, radiating tenderness.

"You know I'm eighteen," Phe grumped, crossing her arms and frowning so deeply it felt her lips were at risk of falling off her face. "Don't tell me nonsense about me being young and you, or General Bastion, knowing what's best for me."

Roar sighed and Phe watched thoughts, responses, zip by in his gaze. After a moment of what looked as though he'd decided his approach, he leaned forward and placed his hand on the armchair, a hair's width from Phe. "I see you're set on this."

Phe tracked the movement, realizing, for the first time, he hadn't touched her. Not once. Which was unlike Roar. For the last eight years, he had always bumped a shoulder or an elbow or made physical contact in some way. He'd grouch some nonsense about safe touch and touch being healing when she'd been younger, and now the absence of it hollowed her.

Even though, Phe knew, any touch right now—after *that*—she didn't want. She had the sudden, overwhelming urge to get up and run. The need to burn off the anxiety and shame and fear that had seeped into her muscles and tendons and organs.

"I've come to understand General Bastion may have implied that this mission was to test your ability to maintain your Lady Orphne persona in case there was a time you needed to if Her Grace was in danger."

He did more than imply.

"He is aware a situation in which you must maintain your Lady Orphne persona while Her Grace is in danger is highly unlikely, nulling this test." Some of the gentleness bled from his gaze.

Phe pouted with commitment. Roar wasn't saying what she hadn't known. Her life purpose was to make sure Kyra was safe, and she viewed every mission and training session within that lens. A failure was unacceptable because that may mean, she might fail Kyra.

But that wasn't the point of this mission.

This mission was about stopping greedy, evil people from doing horrible things to others. This mission was about saving Oriana. It was about the foal, with its mutilated and broken, broken body. It was about every person they'd taken—the girls and boys, children and adults, and forced into their human trafficking—and freeing them.

It was not about preserving her already-broken self.

Phe stiffened, white knuckling the armchair. "I will not abandon these people. I am staying."

Roar's sigh dropped his shoulders a millimeter.

"Okay, then this is the deal." Phe heard a defeated acceptance in his response. His eyes took on a calculating glint. "We'll give you five more days to figure out the other players, see if you can find anything on the grounds. You'll leave us updates at the shed with the foal. After that, you're out, no matter what, and I will personally contact Her Grace and get those orders to ensure this."

Phe's brows pulled tight. How could he bring Kyra into this?

"I will forcibly extract you if that's what it takes. And if you have another spacing, as you call it, you're out immediately."

Phe grunted, knowing he heard her displeasure, annoyance, and anger in the sound. Aggravated that he'd bested her.

"*Fine*," she ground out, determined to get the information they needed before her time was up. Since she'd already been here two days, that meant a total of seven days she'd be in the General's clutches. "Five more days from today," she clarified.

Roar gave a sharp nod then disappeared over the balcony railing.

Phe stood; her jaw set with determination and purpose. She was fighting to give each person taken a new dawn, and nothing was going to stop her from completing her mission. Not even herself.

Not a second after Roar departed, Willa stomped into the room.

"I see you're back with us, princess," Willa called on her way to the closet. Those were the most words Willa had strung together since their unfortunate meeting. "Get up. You've got to change into your nightclothes."

Phe stared at Willa, letting her words wash over her. Whatever outward defiance Phe'd had seconds ago drained from her, stealing the steel in her spine. Her shoulders caved forward, and she wrapped an arm around her waist, and if Willa were closer, she'd have seen Phe's hands shaking.

She dropped, boneless, into the chair as if the effort of standing had sapped all her energy.

She took a moment to track Willa under the disguise she was mustering strength. If she'd left, Seskel would have killed her. Willa may be a bulldog, and in Phe's opinion, she'd definitely made poor decisions along her life path, but she didn't deserve to die. Nor did Willa's family and friends.

Hauling herself from the armchair, Phe stood. Her vision spotted.

It always shocked her how her body reacted to her transformation into her Lady Orphne persona. The aches and weakness and trembles, those were real. The tightness in her chest, the clawing worry in her veins, real.

"Snap to it."

When Phe's speed didn't measure up to Willa's satisfaction, Willa tramped to her and, with bruising finality, physically escorted her into the walk-in closet. Phe glanced around the space. Taking up the majority of the closet were hanging dresses of all shapes and colors. A dark blue dress caught her attention. From her vantage point, it looked identical to one of her favorite pieces, and there were others that stuck out, too.

Had he been collecting dresses she wore? The thought soured her belly. Had he made girls wear these dresses? Pretend to be her?

Seas, I hope not. Phe rolled the fabric between her fingers.

"The General has no need for you tonight," she snapped, as if this had somehow personally insulted her. Willa unlaced her dress and petticoats and, even before they'd pooled at Phe's ankles, started on the corset. Willa roughly worked the laces of her bodice, then peeled the undergarments off her. "He'll be entertaining his resident guest."

Oh no! Oriana.

Phe wrapped her shaky arms around her breasts. Gooseflesh sprouted all over her naked flesh. Phe's exposed skin felt raw. At each touch of Willa's fingers, scorching pain erupted, causing her to tense and flinch.

Willa stalked away and returned with a flimsy nightgown. "Arms up."

Phe obeyed.

Willa shoved her body parts through the appropriate holes and pulled the gown down. Delicate straps caught on her shoulders, and cold silk cascaded down the length of her body, scarcely covering her chest and completely exposing her back. The fitted material ended mid-thigh.

Stars, this was horrible. She wore more undergarments.

Phe crossed her arms again, feeling even more exposed. The moment Willa went to sleep, Phe would find pants and a shirt, proper sleuthing clothing. Running around last night in her corset and underwear had been different and a first.

A rush of heat flamed her cheeks as she recalled Roar's comment —they'd had eyes on her since she got here. How had she not felt them watching? Her gut *always* informed her when she was being watched. It was one of her traits that General Bastion loved to test.

"Off to bed with you now." Willa planted a hand on the exposed skin of her lower back, and searing pain radiated through her.

Phe jerked away from her, putting precious inches of distance between them as they made their way to the sleigh bed. She crawled under the heavy weight of the blankets, watching Willa.

Willa paced to a water pitcher and poured a glass, bringing it over and placing it on her nightstand. Then, wordlessly, she retreated to the sofa in the sitting area and silently settled herself in for the night.

While listening to Willa's breathing settle, Phe wrote with her finger on the sheets—a technique Elzac had suggested when Phe adamantly refused to journal. He'd empathized there was a healing quality to writing out one's thoughts and worries. A releasing. A letting go by doing the action—and not that the action had to be ink to paper.

Phe used the time in bed to purge her mind of the last few days, starting with General Bastion making her roll in a mixture of sewage before being tied up and shoved in a barrel—and how the shadows of her past surged and stormed and threatened to rip her to shreds.

When Willa's breathing fell into rhythmic breaths, Phe shifted in the bed, letting the sheets rustle. Willa's breath didn't change; she was asleep.

Satisfied, Phe slipped soundlessly from the bed and into the closet. Methodically, she went through the drawers until she found a bandeau, a camisole she then layered with a sweater, and a pair of thick wool tights.

Barefooted, she crept into Seskel's quarters and systemically went through every nook in his cozy private dining area, in his walk-in closet, then in his bedroom; she skipped his library—as going through each book right now when he could come out of his playroom at any moment didn't seem practical. She'd return to the library when she knew he was otherwise preoccupied.

She found nothing.

No black book.

No journals.

No paperwork to even sort through.

Nothing.

There was, however, a wall-sized portrait of her. The artist had rendered a depiction of her kneeling, hands resting on her thighs, gazing up and into the room. Her eyes were big and vulnerable and somehow submissive.

Gads. Her stomach twisted. She wasn't going to think about how this was the first and last thing he saw each day. Nope.

Seskel's country estate was massive and, unlike last night, there weren't henchman posted outside her door. Phe worked her way through the barren second floor. Out of Seskel's space, she searched for hidden rooms or entryways in addition to thoroughly going through everything—from books to dresser drawers to clothing pockets.

When the sky began to lighten, she stopped her search. Something in her gut would not let her leave the poor foal to starve. With ease, she slipped out of the house, through the grounds, stole more grain, filled a bucket of water, and even found a carrot in the main stables.

There were no guards posted to watch the foal.

She paused outside of the dilapidated stable, scanning the trees surrounding it suspiciously. She didn't *feel* as if she was being watched, but if Roar said she was, then she was. Uneasiness at not sensing anything chilled her sweat. Slowly, she pushed on the wood door she'd left cracked, whispering,

"Shhhh, baby. It's me again." The noxious smell of the stall hadn't suddenly disappeared, and tears sprung to her eyes at its intensity.

The foal stumbled to its feet, a red glimmer rolling over its eyes for the briefest moment, and it emitted its weird grumble-growl-shriek.

Phe was squeezing herself through the crack in the door, only to freeze at the red. Her heart tried to free itself from her chest, and all the hairs rose on her body. Gulping breaths, she released a barrage of words. "High seas, that red glimmer scares the ever-loving water right out of me."

Phe shuddered. "It's just the only times I've seen red like yours is right before a horde of death-defying, bloodthirsty monsters descended on me—and to be honest, I'm still not sure how in the stars I survived. I'm pretty sure your red is more a figment of my imagination, but it's heart stopping. Literally," Phe punched her chest twice to emphasize, "stops."

Breathing out deeply, she lassoed her heart and wrestled it until it wasn't going to claw through from her ribcage. "I'm sorry I scared you, but I've decided I have to help you."

Wide, white-rimmed eyes watched her. The foal held itself stock still.

Phe fought with the door for a moment to get the water bucket in. Decelerating every move, she kept on rambling in soothing tones. "I don't have much time, so this will be faster than I like." Phe crept closer to where she'd set up her hidden water and grain spots, resupplying them.

Leaving the bucket and satchel she'd taken outside, Phe inched to the foal's side, ignoring the racing of her heart. With a steadying breath, she offered it the carrot she'd found. They stared at each other, each in their own corners, assessing. Neither of them moved.

"You need a name. I can't keep calling you it or baby or foal or horse in my head." Phe's outstretched hand was getting tired. She peeked at its sex. "How's Ava?"

The foal reared her head as if she'd hit it.

"Okay then, not Ava." Phe bit her lip to hold in her smile. "What about Mae?"

If a half-dead, badly beaten, emaciated foal could frown with her whole body, that's what this one was doing.

Phe tossed the carrot in with the grains. The fast movement caused the foal to shuffle backward and flinch. Phe grimaced. "Sorry."

Phe's stomach was rolling, and even though the smell was bad in here, she knew it wasn't that. She needed to get back. "I have to go. I can't let them catch me."

The sun broke the horizon when Phe, freshly clean and with a racing heart, slid into those crisp satin sheets. As she grappled with calming her heart, the door to Seskel's room opened.

Willa startled awake with a snort.

"Shh. Don't wake her," Seskel said in an almost-whisper. "You can go." She heard his soft tread approaching. The bed, on the opposite side of Phe, dipped.

Phe's heart sprinted into her stomach, ultra-aware of the ridiculous slip of a nightgown she'd just put back on.

He crawled over the covers, aligned his body with hers, wrapped an arm around her waist and tucked her tight, then burrowed his nose into her hair.

Phe held utterly still, every nerve in her body flaring.

"Breathe, Orphne," he muttered sleepily, lips brushing her ear.

9

Phe stared at herself in the mirror while she deliberately took an absurd amount of time to lather her hands in soap. She flicked a quick glance to Willa. Willa's left eye twitched. Breathing in her smile, because irritating the daylights out of Willa had become her new pastime, she returned her gaze to the mirror, letting her thoughts stray to Seskel. He'd been absent all day today, as he had yesterday. Was this his routine or happenstance? What did he do all day long? It was getting close to dinner, would he show up after, like he had last night?

She stifled a frustrated sigh. She was three days into this mission and had only discovered the location to Seskel's private playroom. She needed to uncover so much more. She blinked, refocusing her attention to the mirror, and taking in her measure.

Honey-colored eyes stared back at her. Tired wrinkles creased the corners of her eyes, darkening the skin of her eyelids. If Kyra were here, she'd point out how the latest style in makeup does this and how Phe was lucky to have it naturally occur. There was nothing natural about this look—it came from not sleeping for two days in a row and constantly being on high alert.

Willa cleared her throat behind her—the noise filled with annoyance—leaned in, and turned the water on. "Rinse."

Gads, I miss Kyra . . . and Jallia. Neither of those two women would ever treat someone with open disdain, hostility, and impatience. The warm water felt luxurious while she slowly rinsed her hands.

"Enough." Willa turned the faucet off, her temper getting the best of her. "The General wants to have his supper with you. You need to greet him when he comes in."

Phe harrumphed. Immediately, apprehension knotted her stomach, and the back of her throat ached. *Stars, why did she have to see him before dinner?*

Willa gripped her forearm, deliberately making skin-to-skin contact. Pain scorched Phe, and she bit into her inner check. A lot could be said about Willa, but dumb would not be on the list.

"Get in there," Willa seethed, physically yanking Phe toward the door.

Phe shoved the subtly emerging part of warrior Phe back into the shadows of her Lady Orphne persona—feeling more and more like she was cramming her foot into shoes two sizes too small—and her body and mind changed. Trembles returned to her hands, her breathing shallowed, and fear skittered alongside the pain of Willa's touch.

Flaccidly, she let herself be dragged through the golden suite to Seskel's private dining area. With her free hand, she smoothed the exquisite navy-blue satin dress Willa had outfitted her in, trying to not worry about the amount of skin it revealed. The balcony doors were wide open, and the repulsive scent of Seskel's azalea garden drifted in.

The table was on the balcony. The immaculate, delicate settings displayed swirls of floral designs. *Gads, is that more azaleas?* Two red roses adorned the middle of the table, and the water glasses were filled. Beady drops of condensation clung to the crystal.

Willa released her, and Phe wandered to the balcony banister. Gripping its rail, she quickly spotted the hawk, its presence reassuring.

Sighing, she pushed away from the banister and scanned the room. Willa was standing by the door that led into Seskel's library, no doubt waiting for him obediently, and glowering at Phe. It had to be said. The woman had a ferocious glower.

Phe strolled to the table and fingered a fork, denying the urge to pocket it. She didn't want to spend any time with Seskel, especially not a meal filled with his chatter.

What Phe really wanted to do was to check on Oriana, which was an impossible task with Willa hound dogging her steps. And, of course, she had no idea what Seskel's torture schedule was. She could easily be caught if the timing was wrong, and she couldn't risk that.

The door opened in a flourish, and Seskel strode in, adjusting the tie at his neck. Like her, he'd dressed for the occasion. He'd donned one of his ultra-expensive, fitted black suits, a white collar sticking out its top, with a red tie. Dark brown eyes scanned her from head to toe. To Willa, he asked, "Has she eaten?"

"She ate lunch, sir. Picked at her breakfast only."

"Did you ask her why she wasn't eating? Was it the breakfast itself she didn't like? I've heard conflicting accounts of her eating everything and also being very picky."

"I did not, sir."

"Orphne, why didn't you eat breakfast?" Seskel asked pointedly.

Because my stomach was a mess after being spooned by you. She cleared her throat and meekly replied, "I wasn't hungry, General."

Seskel's intense gaze fastened on Willa. "Willa, you will ask from now on," he said crisply. "Is she drinking enough?"

Phe returned her gaze to the fork and debated using it, though she was unsure on who—Seskel or Willa. It shouldn't come as a surprise Seskel was interrogating Willa about her. He had rules about her taking care of herself, and the only way he'd know if she followed them was Willa. But it felt intrusive and violating.

"She looks tired."

"Must be her sickness, sir."

"Have you asked her how she feels?" Worry crept into his voice, and Phe felt the weight of his attention settle on her again.

"No, sir."

"Hm." Seskel loaded his huff with disappointment, then, with steel in his voice. "Ask."

"Lady Orphne, how are you feeling?" Willa complied immediately.

Phe flicked her glance between the two. "Unwell."

Gazing at Seskel from under her lashes, she watched him toy with the cuff of his suit and slid a small butter knife from the table, slipping it under her amulet. It didn't fit.

"Orphne, I'm sorry," he acknowledged. To Willa, he said, as if to explain, "She was taken from her treatment. It's most likely her regiment wasn't complete. Did she have any nightmares last night?"

"None that woke me, sir."

Seas. Would he cease with the questions? A flush crept up Phe's exposed chest and into her neck, like a rising tide. Phe brought both hands to her chest to cover her embarrassment and slipped the knife deep into her corset.

"What did she do all day?"

"She painted, read, sir."

"Did she speak to you?"

"Not a word, sir."

Seskel was halfway across the room, his predatory focus on Phe, when he said. "You're dismissed—be ready to return after dinner."

Phe pressed her elbows into her sides, making herself as small as possible. It'd been one thing when he'd been across the room and she'd been salty from her time with Willa. It was completely different now that he'd closed in on her. He touched her waist, his hand traveling up her bare arm, and dropped a kiss on her collarbone. She couldn't stop her shoulders from stiffening as a fresh explosion of agony rocked her. Or ignore the stabbing pain in her head that had her left eye watering. Or keep her hands from trembling.

"Yes, sir," Willa said, turning to the door. A knock reverberated into the room right before she opened it. Phe caught the outline of a male servant, standing stiffly at attention and blocking Willa's exit.

She felt Seskel smile. His lips pressed into her burning flesh. "Yes, Augustine?"

"Sir, your parents have just arrived."

Seskel's head swung up in surprise. His body tensed. "Have they?"

"Yes, sir. They ordered the cook to make them dinner and announced they are staying the night. Proclaiming they haven't seen you in a while, sir. They also advised the staff that possibly one or both of you brothers could be joining as well."

Seskel dragged in a breath, infused with frustration. "Thank you, Augustine. Please tell them I will be down in a moment."

"Should I tell them you're bringing a guest?" The uncertainty in Augustine's question revealed itself on the last word.

"No, Augustine. My lovely companion will not be joining me, and her presence here is," Seskel cleared his throat, as if to buy a time to choose the right word, "confidential."

"Yes, sir. May I be dismissed?" Augustine asked.

"Yes. Willa." Seskel interlaced his fingers with Phe, setting off another round of agonizing pain. Willa stayed where she was, and Augustine disappeared. "I'll need you to serve my mother."

"Yes, sir, who should I ask to watch over *her*?"

Seskel tugged Phe into the room. "No one. I will leave her in the playroom. I can't risk my mother snooping. You know how she is."

Willa trailed behind them, hesitant to go since he hadn't dismissed her.

This would give her an opportunity with Oriana. This was what she wanted. Yet her gut clenched at being left in the playroom. Phe didn't know what to think. It couldn't be that simple.

"Willa, please wipe any trace of Orphne from the golden room. Then attend to my mother," Seskel said, already tipping the book, *Forbidden Pleasures*.

"Yes, sir," Willa said, disappearing immediately.

The playroom door swung open. Oriana twitched on the bed, but Phe didn't have time to take her in because Seskel led her straight to the cage.

Every muscle tensed in Phe's body. She dug her heels in and tried to yank her hand free. She was not going in there. Palpitations rocked her chest, and a cold sweat broke out all over.

Seskel hauled her close. She smelled his crisp aftershave as they tussled. Phe twisting and wiggling and—

"Stop. You'll hurt yourself," Seskel grunted, trying to subdue her. "You are going in there, Lady Orphne."

The knee Phe was jerking upward and the kidney punch she was aiming to give melted the moment he called her Lady Orphne. All the fight left her. Lady Orphne wouldn't be able to hurt him. Lady Orphne would only squirm, scratch maybe. She sagged, becoming a dead weight, and it didn't faze him.

Her body was engulfed in torturous fire from all their points of contact.

"Had I known you had an aversion to cages," Seskel huffed, swinging the metal door wide, "I'd have punished you with this the other night." He shoved her in, slamming the door shut. The lock clicked.

Phe stayed where she landed, lips clamped shut. Her heart was in her throat and trying to escape through her mouth, along with a scream. Wide eyes met Seskel's, who'd crouched in front of the cage and was running fingers through his disheveled hair.

"Interesting." He quirked his head to the side, eyes curious and knowing. "You've been in one before."

All Phe could do was stare at him. Her chest heaved, and her arms trembled so much, she wasn't sure they would hold her up.

"I'm definitely going to revisit this." Seskel stood, straightened his jacket and tie, patted the cage, and flicked a glance over at Oriana. "I'll be back as soon as I can."

Phe tracked him across the room. The moment the door shut, she dug the butter knife out of her corset with quivering and weak fingers. She needed to get out of here. Shakily, she crawled to the lock and jabbed the knife in, but she was shaking so much, she couldn't feel the mechanism.

The knife slipped from her fingers, clattering to the floor outside the cage.

White knuckling the cold metal bars and leaning her forehead into them, her eyes trained on the knife. She forced herself to go through the infuriating process of the four-count breaths. When she could suck an unstilted breath in, she slithered her arm through the bars, straining to feel the warmed metal of the knife.

A fingertip touched it.

Her nail scraped the surface, trying to pull it closer.

It tilted toward her.

She tried again, this time, a little more of her fingertip made contact.

It moved toward her. She repeated the motion until she could get a second and third finger on it. Then she wrapped her hand around it. With a deep breath in, she heaved herself onto her knees and positioned the knife in the lock. Even though her heart boomed loudly in her ears, her hand was steady, and the release of the lock sounded explosive.

The door swung open.

Phe lunged out and half-crawled, half-ran until the bed stopped her. Dropping her head into her hands, she rocked, sucking in one long breath after another. *High Seas. Oh, flipping high seas.* If Bastion knew she would react like that, he'd throw her into a cage and walk away. *Gads, he can never find out.*

Inhale, exhale. Inhale, exhale. *Gads, I have to go back in . . . don't think about it now.*

Think about the mission. Both hands fisted around the butter knife for dear life. *Oriana.*

Prying her fingers apart, she slid the knife into her corset again, then flipped around and climbed onto the bed.

Oriana was huddled in between two pillows with the sheet wrapped around her. The ankle straps had been removed, but she still wore the wrist ones. Her pallor was the same, but Phe could see a few fresh bruises on the parts of her that were exposed. The stiffness in which Oriana held herself told Phe she hadn't escaped the lashes.

Even though everything she saw told her this girl was anything but okay, she forced the only question that came to mind through clenched teeth. "Are you okay?"

Oriana swallowed, blinked repeatedly, and gave her chin a few soft shakes. No.

Phe nodded, expecting that answer and digging around in her brain for what else to ask. The fear that had clouded her mind was slowly settling, not gone, but giving her the slightest space for thoughts to occur.

Licking her lips, she compelled her voice to work. "I'm Phe." Silence took over. *Gads, I'm horrible at this.* Why could she ramble on to a horse, yet couldn't speak more than a few words to another human?

Phe folded herself into a cross-legged position, watching Oriana's skin ripple in flinches. Closing her eyes and envisioning the beaten foal, Phe said, "I won't hurt you."

After a long silence, she said, "Do you know how long you've been here?" She didn't know where to start with her questions or even if asking her about her stay was a good idea.

Oriana gave the same stilted chin movements.

There were too many overlaying healing and fresh bruises to guess. "Can you tell me how you got here?"

Tears welled in Oriana's eyes, and this time she sucked her bottom lip into her mouth. Phe shifted her gaze from Oriana's to reexamine the room. Phe'd had trouble looking into people's eyes—and still did when she was mixing with the Oceanid elite. It was only people she was comfortable with who she could hold gazes.

"Why are you talking to me?" Oriana's voice wavered like a leaf caught in a tumult of wind.

"Because I want to help you, but I don't know how," Phe admitted.

"You can't help me," came Oriana's whisper-soft reply. "I'm going to die in here, and so are you."

"Not if I can help it," Phe said, counting the striation marks on Oriana's neck. Ten. And there were fingerprint bruises, too. A jolt of adrenaline shot through her, and invisible wounds on her neck throbbed.

Oriana didn't respond, her disbelief permeating the air.

Phe scrubbed her hand over her face. *I'm so bad at this.* Sliding off the bed, she stood stiffly and then rolled her shoulders. Fear had a way of seizing all her muscles. She took another deep breath. "I'm trying to save us both."

Phe wandered past the studded wall. She couldn't start her search there. In the room Grum had kept her, there'd been similar stubs that he used to hang her from. Instead, she rifled through everything. The racks, the dresser, the drawers, shoved her arm under the mattress, books, all of Seskel's devices. She looked under the rugs. Searched under the cage, the bed, and tapped on every inch of the walls. Any place there could be a hidey hole.

She came up empty-handed.

"What are you doing?" Oriana asked nervously.

Phe crossed her arms, feeling filthy from touching everything. "Looking for anything that can incriminate him." She gave Oriana a rueful smile. "I was really hoping he had a little black book he kept with a list of all the names of those he works with and who he's taken over the years and to whom he sold them."

"There are others?"

Phe nodded, scrunching up her face.

"Oh." The sheet rustled around Oriana as she pulled it tighter.

Phe perched on the bed and hung her head. "I'm sorry this is happening to you because you have a resemblance to me."

Oriana sniffed, her voice feather light, "It's not your fault. It's Jeremy's."

"Who's Jeremy?" Phe brows crinkled. Was he one of Seskel's foot soldiers?

Oriana said—almost incomprehensibly—around a sob, "He was my boyfriend."

It felt as though the weight of the world plummeted on Phe's shoulders. "Your boyfriend?" Oriana nodded her response, tears streaking her cheeks. Oriana had a youthfulness to her that hadn't caught up to her broken innocence yet. "How old are you?"

"Six-six-sixteen."

"And Jeremy, was he sixteen too?"

A sob escaped, and she slumped over, only to hiss and straighten. Oriana nodded her head.

Dread roiled Phe's stomach. "Why is it Jeremy's fault?"

"He sold me. Tricked me into sneaking out with him an-and," another sob, "the men were there waiting with him." She ended on a wail.

Phe took deliberate, measured breaths. How did a sixteen-year-old boy get involved in—no, it didn't matter. Trying to understand the hows and whys of the depths of people's depravities never led to answers. She fought the urge to find out exactly who this Jeremy was so that she could pay him a visit.

Oriana rocked, crying violently.

Phe fiddled with her amulet. Oriana's emotions swelled in the room, and Phe funneled her energy into resisting the powerful tide of joining with them. There was nothing Phe could say to assuage the pain, and even if there was, most likely she'd botch the delivery and make everything worse.

They stayed like this, Phe at the foot of the bed, Oriana huddled at the headboard, for a long time. Long enough for Oriana to stop crying and rocking. Long enough for Phe's back to ache. Long enough for the silence to become companionable.

It was Oriana who broke it. "I worry about my parents."

Phe glanced sharply at her, not expecting this.

Oriana snuffled and used the sheet—already spotted with her tears—to wipe her face. She nodded at Phe. "It's just, I'm their only child and . . . I know my absence is killing them, and I don't—." Oriana hiccupped. "I don't think my mom will survive."

Phe's why must have been written all over her face, because instead of waiting for Phe to ask it, Oriana answered it.

"My parents, they always wanted lots and lots of children. They tried, and every single one they lost and buried except for me."

Oriana took a shaky breath before continuing. "When I was born, alive, they thought it was a miracle. Mom used to tell me that, every morning while she was pregnant with me, she'd wake up to see the sunrise. And every morning she'd pray for the miracle of me."

Phe's heart twisted. How she'd wished her mother would have loved her in the same way. Being an orphan with no memories prior to Grum, she'd never know if her parents had cared. This longing—to know who her parents are, to know what happened and why she'd ended up where she did—came only when others talked like this and reminded her of the loss.

A watery smile formed on Oriana's face. "It's why they called me Oriana. I am their miracle, their sunrise." Her chin wobbled, and she swallowed audibly. "Mom said I was a challenging birth, but Dad tells me when she's not around that Mom almost died from it. I know Mom acts really tough, but I see the pain she's hiding, and I know that losing me will literally kill her."

Gads. How many others were in this same situation because of Seskel?

"And I keep holding onto that. If I die, Mom will too, but it's so hard." Oriana stared at the racks. "What he's done to me . . ." Her breath shuddered. "I don't know how I can live after this."

Even though it wasn't a question, it was an area Phe had a lot of experience with. She cleared her throat and stood, her heart bristling with unease at her intention. "I used to live one breath at a time, and eventually those stacked up into a day. Then another. I didn't live for me. I lived for my best friend," Phe admitted, hoping Oriana could see the parallel. If she were honest, she still did—but that wasn't the point. As she neared the cage, her heart sped up.

"You've lived through something like this before?" Horror radiated from every syllable.

Phe was so close to the metal cage she could rest her hand on it. Her heart beat at her chest cavity—trying to break free—her stomach knotted, and everything in her screamed at her not to go back in. She turned a sad smile onto Oriana. "There's no way you'll be the same person you came in here as. You'll be the person who survived this. There's so much power in that, even on all the messy days."

Phe captured Oriana's gaze, hovering at the cage's gaping opening. "Will you tell him?"

Oriana shook her head, no.

Phe closed her eyes, stepped into the cage, and closed the door behind her. She bit her inner cheek so hard she tasted the coppery tang of her blood.

"Maybe, maybe I'll live for my mom and our sunrises," Oriana murmured, her voice softening to the point it was almost hard to hear.

The door to the library clicked, then silently opened.

A beaming Seskel strode in with a Cheshire grin. He'd replaced the suit he'd worn with causal clothes, and his eyes twinkled. He took a moment to close the door, as if trying to measure the room's emotional temperature. When he closed the door, he stayed where he was, flicking his gaze between Phe and Oriana.

The air became pressurized.

"My parents," Seskel announced, while sauntering toward the bed, "have decided to return to their estate tonight. It is unfortunate they interrupted our dinner plans, Orphne." When he reached the bedside, he grabbed the chain to Oriana's wrist and tugged her to him. Oriana was half-dragged and half-crawled until she was at the edge in front of him, eyes pinned to the ground.

The sheet Oriana had wrapped around her fell, and Phe's gaze became riveted to her back, where there was a mishmash of angry red scabs from her shoulder blades to just above her buttocks. No wonder she couldn't slouch.

Seskel ran his hands up her arms, then captured her neck. "What have you told her?"

"We-we didn't ta-talk, G-gen-eral," Oriana sputtered around gasps, her hands limply clinging to his, seemingly more out of instinct than an attempt to pull him off.

"I'm not worried about her talking." Seskel's predatorial gaze landed on Phe. "But you."

"No-no-nothing, Gen-gen-eral." Her gasps were getting shorter, and the strain on her back caused some scabs to start bleeding.

Phe gripped the metal bars, the butter knife jabbing into her, reminding her of its presence.

Seskel's eyes narrowed on Phe. He released one hand from Oriana's neck, only to unbuckle his belt. With quick movements, he had the belt wrapped around one hand. His other hand still choked her.

High seas. Phe's stomach dropped and her whole body shook. *What can I do?*

Seskel tossed her aside and brought the belt down on the back of her thigh with a resounding crack. Oriana's cry was muffled in the bedding.

"Stop!" Phe yelled, shaking the metal caging.

Surprisingly, Seskel did.

He strode to the cage and scowled into it.

"Stop, General," she muttered. Phe swallowed, her mind running in circles, and shuffled away from the bars. What had she been thinking, speaking? Lady Orphne wouldn't have.

Those dark eyes caressed her face, and his own features softened. "Orphne." There was a sacredness with which he said her name. "How are you feeling?"

"Unwell, General."

Seskel scrunched his mouth. "Do you need more of your treatments?"

"I think so, General," Phe answered, keeping her gaze on his right earlobe.

"Do you know how they were treating you?"

"No, General," Phe shook her head, reciting what she normally told people. "My doctor only speaks to General Bastion about my care and sickness."

"Problematic, but we'll figure it out." Seskel palmed his chin, eyes hooding as he contemplated something. He dug a hand into his pocket, brandishing a key. "I wanted you to watch, but you haven't eaten dinner and look piqued." He pushed the cage door aside and offered Phe his hand.

Clenching her teeth, she grabbed it. He hauled her into his chest, tangling a hand in her hair and holding her flush against him. Every nerve ending burst into painful awareness.

Seskel released her, interlacing their fingers again. "Come. Willa is waiting for you with your dinner."

As he led her from the room, Phe's gaze connected with Oriana's and she mouthed, "I'm sorry," putting her heart and soul into the words and knowing they weren't enough.

10

That night, Phe crept through the trees on the outskirts of Seskel's property. The satchel she'd stolen rubbed heavily against her thigh, filled with more grain, an apple and a carrot, and a bottle of water.

The skeletal paddock was just ahead, and she was getting glimpses of the vast night sky above it.

Wide, fear-filled, honey-colored eyes filled Phe's vision, and she had to blink, yet again, until they disappeared. Her stomach sloshed uncomfortably, storming with the waves of guilt cresting Phe, and an ache took up residence at the base of her throat. How could she have allowed herself to be dragged away from Oriana? How could she let Seskel continue to hurt Oriana while she pretended to be weak?

The wrongness of it all slithered under her skin.

If General Bastion had allowed me—

She stopped the thought. It was no use wishing General Bastion had given her a different set of orders. She'd agreed to stay in her Lady Orphne persona knowing it wouldn't be easy. What she hadn't realized was how much harder it would become once she met others and couldn't do anything to help them.

Her skin tingled uncomfortably. It felt as if there was something within her trying to fight its way free from the barrier of her skin—

yet she couldn't figure out what it was. Guilt. Disgust. Dread. Fear. It also seemed to mingle with determination, and a driving need to protect Oriana, and this foal, and the others who were taken.

Gads, this is the worst mission ever.

She paused at the last tree to scan the area.

The guilt chiseling away at her innards for leaving Oriana alone with Seskel was wrecking her. The only reason she was here and not there was because it wasn't just about Oriana. Phe couldn't make this about Oriana.

It had to be about the bigger picture.

Phe stepped through a portion of the fencing, plunked the ladened bag down, and placed her hands on her hips. Leaning back, she glared into the night sky.

Stars speckled its canvas. It was beautiful, but nothing close to Uklesa's famous terrace, Gateway To The Stars, which overlooked the Sryln Sierras. Phe had a portrait, called *Ascension,* that captured the essence of it hanging in her room in House Nereid.

Phe gulped in large lungfuls of fresh hair. *I'm as bad as Willa.* Phe's stomach, already a knotted mess, gave her a confirmatory squeeze. *Oriana can last a few more days.* She had to, because when Roar extracted Phe, Oriana was coming, too.

And so was this foal. It was that simple.

Phe dropped her chin to her chest, preparing for the wretched stench, and inched through the slot in the door. The smell hit her, uncaringly, but unlike last night, her entrance cued a cloud of flies, their buzz vibrating the air. There was no red glimmer. There was no weird grumble-growl-shriek or clinking chain.

Oh stars, have they killed her? Am I too late?

Phe closed her eyes, willing them to adjust faster to this darkness. It didn't help. She schooled her voice into a waterfall of soothing tones. "Baby, you okay?" she called out as she shuffled forward on the mushy ground.

A fly buzzed in her ear.

Phe halted midway through the stall, her vision clearing enough to see the outline of the foal's body. She startled and shifted and fleetingly tried to get up.

Phe could see one of her white eyes. Phe dropped to her knees and crawled to the foal.

She tried to move away from Phe, backing into the wall, but there was no give, and the movement seemed to hurt the foal. Phe gripped her thighs, grimly looking over a new network of lashes.

"Oh baby," she breathed, heart aching. "They came back. I was really hoping—" She blew out a frustrated breath. "It doesn't matter what I was hoping. I brought more food."

Phe retrieved the satchel and resettled. With meticulously slow movements, she unpacked it. When the foal didn't make a move to eat, she broke the carrot into pieces and held it to her mouth. The hair on the foal's nose tickled her palm, and her breath cascaded in warm puffs. They stayed like this for countless minutes. Phe refused to give up. The foal needed to eat.

Then the foal's dry muzzle brushed her hand, and the carrot disappeared.

Phe repeated this until the whole carrot was gone. Then, she switched to the apple. The water was harder, and she ended up drizzling more of it on the foal's muzzle than into her mouth.

"I'm so sorry. I promise when I leave, I'll get you, too," Phe said, righting the food bowl and pouring the rest of the grain into it. She had to search for the water bowl. It had gotten knocked around by whoever had come in and hurt the foal. She filled it, leaving both close.

"I'll come back with more tomorrow," Phe stated, then asked, "What about naming you Lux?"

The horse snorted.

"How about Hope?"

The foal raised her muzzle as if she were snubbing her nose at Phe.

"Hope would've been a good one. You know, with the situation. Do you feel the same way about Faith?"

The foal ignored her.

"I've never met a horse like you," Phe said, collecting the bag and empty bottle. "And I think I understand why they're so scared of you."

Phe got to her feet, the foal watching her intently. "People are scared of things that are different. You're different. I'm different. Sometimes I wonder, is being different ultimately sparing us somehow? Do our differences—even though they cause us seas of anguish—ultimately save us?"

Phe hovered, half-in, half-out of the shed, caught on the thought. Had being different *saved* her? It hadn't saved her from Grum, but the last eight years with Kyra and General Bastion . . . If her differences hadn't intrigued General Bastion—even though he was a bastard—he'd have enforced sending her to Seabreak orphanage. Instead, he trained her, and it was in those sessions she started to come alive. It was in those sessions she'd found inner and outer strength. It was in those sessions, because of the sweat and blood and pain, she'd found endurance, resilience, and bravery.

Phe's skin tingled. Had everything she gone through so far, Grum included, spared her from a worse fate? Phe sucked in a semi-clean breath, then expelled the thought. There was no use pondering that line of questions; only the stars knew those answers.

"Try to stay alive for a few more days," she said over her shoulder as she emerged into a symphony of crickets.

Phe took out the paper on which she'd jotted a quick note to Shadow Unit on and found a decent-sized rock to hide it under. It was the best she could do. Bone weary, she set off toward the mansion.

11

The coppery tang of blood filled her mouth again as she bit into her inner cheek. Where Seskel rested his hand, all she could feel was pain. Scorching, bone-searing pain that radiated in ripples along the raw nerves of her vertebra. You'd think it would have lessened over the last few days with the amount of touching Seskel'd done. It hadn't. It had gotten worse.

And, after last night, seeing Oriana and the foal, Phe knew it could be so much worse.

It had been two days since Roar's visit, four days in total since she'd arrived. That meant she only had three more days. She could do it. She would do it. Even if it meant taking them one breath at a time.

Today, Seskel broke his pattern and showed up mid-afternoon, escorting her for the first time out of her suite. He tensed his fingers on Phe's lower back, digging them in slightly—and jolting her with another punch of pain—to guide her toward his grand stairway. They descended slowly, the mansion spewing opulence and etiquette and lies, and strolled through its splendid hallways until Seskel ushered her into a private parlor.

A man lounged on the couch.

He had trim, black, wiry hair, and a pair of thick, round, black eyeglass frames perched on his flat nose. The glasses made his unusual green eyes appear bigger, giving the impression he was the studious type.

He'd made himself at home on the dark brown leather couch, an ankle crossed over his knee and one arm resting across the back of the sofa while he sipped from a glass filled with golden liquid. His green gaze feasted on her, smoldering with a repulsive darkness, then it locked onto Seskel's over the rim of the crystal glass he held.

Instantly, everything Phe knew about him gushed like a broken dam.

Nisroc Aldes.

Nisroc was a retired military man who worked for the Brevil's family business in importing and exporting. The hairs raised on Phe's neck.

Gads, were they smuggling people out of Xafara? Her stomach rolled.

About a year ago, Cithias had introduced him to Kyra, and by extension, Phe—just after he'd been hired—at a charity event. Cithias had boasted about snatching him up, as if he'd been a rare white stag. A trophy hire. He'd raved over Nisroc's extensive military service and how far he'd come after leaving Seabreak orphanage, where he'd grown up. Cithias had gone on to rave about Nisroc's astuteness within the industry, his vast contacts on the mainland, and his passion for working with orphaned children. His way of giving back, she recalled him saying.

Oh, high seas and stars, he has access to the orphanage. Bitterness scoured Phe's stomach. *What was he doing to those children?*

"You brought her?" Nisroc cocked his head, his left eyebrow tensed, and his tone dripped with displeasure.

He signed his fate the moment he spoke, identifying himself as the Colonel.

Seskel ignored him, leading Phe to the sofa opposite him. "Sit," he commanded her, then to Nisroc. "A fire?"

"Yes, General," Phe whispered, sinking into the lush, leather cushion. She trained her gaze to the floor and let her shoulders collapse, watching the men from under her lashes. She bit into her inner cheek again, gnashing the pulverized flesh between her teeth. He was not a general. He was despicable. Loathsome. And each time she called him General, she despised him more and more.

Heat from the fireplace warmed her cheek. Its flames licked up the magnificent stonework, the tips lost behind the decadent mantle.

The edges of Nisroc's mouth lifted in amusement.

Seskel laughed self-consciously. "Ignore that." He headed toward a table with a decanter and glasses on it. "Your obsession with fire rivals mine with Orphne. Need a refill?"

Nisroc's gaze hooded, and he brought his glass to his lips. "Bring the decanter with you. Aren't we celebrating?"

Seskel beamed a smile so bright, it hid the vileness of his face. "Business first."

"Hmm," Nisroc muttered dubiously, taking a slow sip from his glass.

Seskel deposited the decanter on a nearby table and sank into the couch next to Phe. He splayed his legs wide, pinning his leg to Phe's, and leaned forward, filling his glass. The woodsy, sweet scent of bourbon poured into the room. When he was satisfied, he reclined into the sofa and draped his free arm along the back of the couch, skimming Phe's shoulders with a finger.

Phe couldn't suppress her shudder.

Nisroc perused Phe slowly, the weight of his gaze hungry and dark.

Seskel tipped his glass at Nisroc in salute but stiffened when he noticed where Nisroc's attention lay. "Nisroc," he snapped viciously, his bourbon spilling.

Nisroc whipped his gaze to Seskel, surprise arching his brows, indignation spiking his words. "You're not going to share?"

Seskel's fingers wove into Phe's hair, pressing her head into his chest. "She's different. You know that."

Phe forced herself to take small swigs of air into her frozen lungs. Her body shook with the movement. In: one, two, three, four. Out: one, two, three, four. In: one. *I'm doing this for Oriana.* Two. *The horse.*

Three. *Countless victims* Four. *Kyra.* Out: one. *They'll be punished.* Two. *I can hurt them.* Three. *I am in control.* Four. *This will not kill me.*

From his shocked expression, Nisroc didn't appear to have known that. "What I know is we've always shared."

Seskel's shrug said he didn't care. "*You* know how special she is to me."

"She's 'special.'" The glint in Nisroc's eyes sharpened and it was like he took the word special and dragged it across a feces-covered floor. "What have you been doing with her for the last five days if she's so precious?"

Seskel appeared completely unconcerned with the waves of aggression Nisroc was shedding. "Establishing the rules and who she belongs to." Seskel peered at Phe, walloping her with the strong, woodsy sweet bourbon coating his breath. "Haven't we, Orphne?"

"Yes, General," Phe mumbled, tucking her free hand under her skirts so she could clench it. The pain had redoubled, and the center of her forehead felt as though she were being stabbed. *Gads, his breath.*

Seskel pressed his lips to her forehead, where she felt him smile at Nisroc. "Don't look so salty. She's not like the others. You know you can join me with them anytime. In fact, after this, we can go upstairs and have some time with Oriana."

Nisroc didn't respond right away. His mouth pulled in fits of twitches and edgy, pouty movements. "I was expecting—" He cut himself off and shook himself as if the anger would release with the movement, only it clung to him. "Never mind. I accept your invitation. Now, to business," he said, his tone clipped. "We need to kill Curo."

Phe froze. *That's not good.*

"Why?" Seskel asked curiously. He released his grasp on Phe's head to play with a strand of her hair.

"An essential stranger waltzed into our organization and demanded a higher position. That's unacceptable."

"Our soldiers know there is a reward for bringing in girls with her resemblance. We've incentivized this from the beginning. Only this time, someone stole her from under House Nereid's guards. Tell me, how can that act alone not require a bigger reward?" Seskel calmly asked.

"Because I'm not sure he did it," Nisroc retorted.

Seskel hooted with laughter. "I can assure you, this is my girl."

"If she was really missing, wouldn't there be news and a country-wide search, with everyone hustling over to Her Grace—including your family—to fake console her, because no one in their right minds actually likes Orphne?"

Seskel's chest expanded, moving Phe with it, but Nisroc growled and kept going. "All I'm saying is my gut is telling me there's something wrong here. From all reports of Her Grace and their friendship, she'd be calling to search every house in Xafara, and who knows if she could find Lady Orphne through her ability." He shuddered with his last words, as if he thought Kyra's ability unnatural. "Compound that with you not *sharing*? And I don't see enough bruises on her that would satisfy your appetite. Something's gravely amiss."

Seas. There was so much wrong with these men, yet none of it seemed to include their wits.

It was Seskel's turn to brood. The steady lub-dub of his heart pounded into Phe's head.

"I hear you. First, I want to point out we've known of Sergeant Curo since we expanded into Xafara. Lieutenant Jetts has kept us well-informed about all of his soldiers. And hasn't he specifically raved about this Curo?" Seskel circled a strand of hair around a finger, tugging it lightly.

"Hmph."

"Right, so, Curo—though a stranger to us in person—we've known of him for some time. Have you considered inviting Lieu-tenant Jetts here to confirm Curo's identity?"

"I already have," Nisroc grumpily replied, aggressively stamping his raised foot to the floor. "He ID'd him three days ago."

"Okay, we've confirmed he's not a stranger to us," Seskel rationally continued. "Who knows why they haven't announced Orphne's miss-ing? It doesn't matter." Seskel took the ends of Phe's hair and swept them on the curve of her collarbone. "I think you disliked him the moment he blocked the doorway and one-upped us, and you just want to kill him. Yeah?"

Nisroc planted his elbows on his knees, interlocking his hands into a ball of tension in front of him. "Yes."

Phe swallowed several times. How could people be so blasé with life? About taking a life?

"Well, why didn't you lead with that?" Seskel clucked. "You and all your drama. It's simple, you don't like him, he's dead. How are we going to do it? I assume you have a plan already."

The tension whooshed out of Nisroc's body, and a slow smile crawled its way up his face. "I sent notifications to all our lieutenants the night of her arrival, mandating everyone's presence to celebrate Curo's promotion." A mean glimmer sparked in his eyes. "We'll kill him in front of everyone to send the message that no one can make demands on us."

Seskel stopped toying with her hair.

Phe peeked at him to see he'd pinned Nisroc with a deadly stare and an even deadlier smile. "I knew I loved you for a reason."

Nisroc huffed, brows bouncing to his forehead. He leaned over and refilled his bourbon. "Not enough to share."

"Deal with it. She's mine." Seskel buried his nose into Phe's hair. "When's it scheduled?"

Nisroc knocked back the shot of bourbon, then refreshed his glass, glowering. "In two days."

"I take it you want to behead him?" Seskel's lips mouthed against her scalp. Cold sweat broke out in Phe's armpits. "Or do you want to burn him?"

"Behead. I figured I'd have Hukir and Jetts hold him." Nisroc reclined into the sofa, resting his glass on his chest. "Pity we can't torture him."

"We'll work that out tonight." Seskel's voice dropped an octave.

Oh, Oriana. Guilt devoured the lining of her stomach. *I'm so sorry!*

"And, if we don't, you should go to the caves after," Seskel continued, tone serious. "We all know what happens when you don't."

The caves? Was that where Seskel and Nisroc kept everyone? Were the caves on the property?

Nisroc huffed dismissively.

"Last thing on my agenda," Seskel said. "Is tomorrow's auction all set?"

"Just the normal minor issues." Nisroc downed the rest of his drink. "Guests have RSVP'd. Rosco and Jazmine have requested to bring new guests, which I declined. Neither has been vetted yet." Nisroc shrugged one shoulder. "Keeping our guest list in mind, I've selected the ones for purchase. We should be all set." Eyeing the way Seskel was rubbing his face into Phe's hair again, Nisroc cleared his throat.

Seskel straightened, roughly dislodging Phe from her forced lean on him, and finished his drink. "Is that it?"

"Yeah." Nisroc stood, his pants stretching tightly over a huge bulge in his groin area. Phe wished she could unsee the sight. "Let's pay Oriana a visit."

12

Dread congealed in her stomach, rolling uneasily, as they strode through the deserted hallways. The heat from Seskel's hand enhanced what felt like molten lava eroding her skin from his touch. The nauseating scent of azaleas perfumed the ground floor, trailing them as they started their ascent of the grand stairway. Phe leaned heavily on the gold encrusted banister; her Lady Orphne persona having eroded her strength.

Phe glanced around Seskel at Nisroc. Lines of displeasure wrinkled the corners of Nisroc's mouth, down-turning it. She flicked her gaze to his eyes and became entrapped by his side-eyed glare—it held a dark promise. Suddenly, she found it hard to breathe. To swallow. She stumbled on a step.

Seskel's arms bracketed her immediately, stabilizing her, his concentrated gaze almost as scorching as his touch. "This, Nisroc, is what I'm talking about. She's too fragile, too weak."

"I see." Nisroc's tone was neutral.

Phe wrapped a trembling arm around her waist, hunched further into herself, and detached from Seskel's steadying hands.

"I've spoken with our physician, she's not available to come until next week to evaluate Orphne."

"You're bringing in Dr. Jorma?" Surprise lightened Nisroc's response.

Seskel shrugged, "Of course. Orphne needs to continue her treatment."

Phe's skin prickled at the mention of Dr. Jorma. Phe knew the doctor because they'd worked side-by-side at fundraisers for Seabreak orphanage and other societal causes that Kyra aligned with. Slowly, they all started up the steps again while Phe grappled with this new information. Seskel had grown up in Seabreak, and the good doctor oversaw the health of the orphanage residents.

A shudder slithered through her, and she discarded the idea. Dr. Jorma served a vast number of families, including the Brevils. It was purely coincidence.

Nisroc coughed. "This whole situation has been anticlimactic."

Seskel ruefully laughed, "Agreed. Oddly, though, I have a different set of urges with her. More . . ." his face puckered. "Protective. Possessive."

"I'm seeing this." Nisroc's voice mirrored Seskel's distaste. "What are you going to do with her? Seems useless and reckless for you to keep her."

They got to the landing and, even though Phe needed to stop and breathe—her lungs were too constricted—she didn't. She couldn't risk stopping and her knees giving out, or the shadows dancing in the periphery of her vision taking over, or the flashes of Grum circling her.

"I am keeping her," Seskel decisively responded, reaching out to grip her arm instinctively, as if Nisroc would try to tear her from him, breaking Phe's flash. "I've waited too long for her, and now that I have her, she isn't going anywhere."

They entered the golden suite.

"Then it seems as though you will have a need to continue to host, which reminds me, there's another lookalike in the caves." Nisroc said as he trailed them to the large chair on the balcony Phe'd been using.

"I've been enjoying my time with Oriana. I'm planning to have

Orphne join us after Dr. Jorma sees her." Seskel said as he guided her into the plush seat. "I've taken her in, but she hasn't reacted well. I'm contemplating how to gradually introduce her to our ways in a way that she will be receptive to and like."

Gads, that will never happen.

"Cripes." Nisroc drifted toward Seskel's suite, derisively saying, "You sound like your fretting old man."

Seskel straightened, an odd, edgy smile on his face. "Willa's in the playroom, readying Oriana for us. Would you let her know she's needed out here?"

Phe dropped her chin to her chest, eyes cast on the balcony floor, fighting the ache in the back of her throat. *I could stop them.* Her Lady Orphne persona surged forward, fear discoloring the lenses of her vision. Her breathing shallowed into sips of guilt-laden air, and her stomach knotted in clumps of dread and self-loathing.

"What do you need Willa for?"

Seskel gave him a pointed, irritated look. "You tell me."

Nisroc shook his head, disapprovingly. "You're ridiculous."

"I know." Seskel's jaw clenched, causing muscles to flex on his face. "Just do it."

Nisroc disappeared, leaving a stream of scorn in his wake.

Seskel leaned forward, cupped her chin, and planted his wet lips on Phe's forehead. "Don't worry, Orphne. I know you had to bury this part of you deep, there is no way Her Grace or any of her household would allow this part of you—the one that craves pain and pleasure—to be free. But I have all the time in the world to coax it out of you. And I will."

Willa entered the room, and he straightened to his full height. "Willa, make sure she eats, and bring me a blanket. She's cold."

"Yes, sir." Willa handed him the blanket.

"We'll be in with my guest all night," Seskel said, tucking a golden-hued quilted blanket around her. When he was done, he tipped her chin up. His blown pupils were encased in a lining of dark brown excitement. "Why don't you watch the sunset and then retire for the night? You look exhausted."

"Yes, General," she whispered.

Seskel glanced over her one more time, then strode to his suite, where Nisroc was leaning on the frame, arms crossed, watching. She locked eyes with Nisroc. If someone's gaze could say *I-plan-to-do-every-vile-nasty-torturous-thing-I-have-in-my-arsenal-to-you,* his did.

Phe lowered her gaze, not missing how Nisroc's expression changed when it alighted onto Seskel. Phe didn't have any experience with what lust looked like, but she was positive that was an ingredient, along with a teaspoon of grimness and a tablespoon of eagerness.

Her stomach recoiled, all the dread and self-loathing and guilt trying to fight its way free. Phe scanned the darkening horizon until she spotted the hawk in a tree. Fixing her gaze on it, she reminded herself, *I'm doing this so Oriana and the others can be free to watch the sunrise.*

Phe let the time pass, thinking about the caves she knew of in Oceanid. There were public caves in the cliffsides to the only beach in Oceanid and Xafara, but those were too public, and they filled with the tide. The rest of Xafara's island was sheer, insurmountable cliffs. She decided to search Seskel's property again, looking specifically for any type of entryway that could lead into a cave system.

Her gut was telling her it wasn't on the property, and there was a chance it wasn't actually a cave. What they referred to as 'the cave' could be a name they called the location and not have anything to do with an actual cave.

With a steadying breath, Phe hauled herself off the armchair.

It was time to use the sleeping tonic on Willa.

Unsteady, as she embodied her Lady Orphne persona, she made her way to the washroom.

"Where are you going?" Willa snapped, rising with her.

Phe glanced between Willa and the washroom.

The connecting door to Seskel's rooms slammed open, whacking loudly against the wall. Phe froze, her innards—her two personas—standing at attention. The warrior Phe had her shift her weight onto her toes, but her Lady Orphne persona surged with the barrage of adrenaline and locked her in place.

"You!" Nisroc stormed out, shirtless and with the top of his pants undone.

Phe's pulse throbbed at her neck and, instinctively, she held her breath, too frightened to move.

Nisroc was on her in seconds. He barreled into her and threw her against the wall, plastering his body over hers, his forearm across her collarbones. His face was so close, they were practically touching noses.

"Nisroc!" Seskel hollered from inside the playroom.

Phe missed nothing. Not the flaring of his nostrils or the death promise in his eyes, or the flush to his cheeks or the blemishes in the pores of his skin, or the hard length pressed into her belly.

Nisroc curled his upper lip grimly, showing blunt, coffee-stained teeth and breathing woodsy-sweet bourbon fire in her face.

Phe pressed her right cheek into the wall, as far from him and his fire-breathing madness as possible. Her fingers dug into the flesh of his arm, and she bit into her raw, chewed-up inner cheek. Grum's voice booming through her, *You are worthless, weak, useless . . .*

With his free hand, Nisroc gripped her bodice and ripped it down the center. Then he started to pull up her skirts, the volume of her petticoats hindering him.

Oh seas, oh seas, oh seas. But the seas were not coming to save her. Nor was her team. Nor would she, because if she did, all the nicely aligned pieces to stop this operation would fall apart.

"Nisroc!"

But if she let him do this, didn't allow her warrior Phe—who pounded to take over with every heartbeat—would *she* fall apart? Could she let Nisroc or Seskel rape her? Violate her in a way Grum never had?

Seskel reached them, wrapping an arm around Nisroc's neck and the other going to the back of his head.

Nisroc twisted and smashed Seskel into the wall next to her.

Phe bolted across the room, stopping when she was huddled

behind the chair, heart pounding. Her head and limbs felt light, airy. With hands that trembled so much she struggled to pick up her torn dress, she smeared the fabric into place.

No. She sucked in a breath and let the power of her decision roll through her. *No.* She was willing to sacrifice a lot for the mission, but she would not sacrifice that part of herself.

She peeked around the side of the chair, Seskel had Nisroc pinned.

She wrapped her hands around her legs and watched Nisroc grunt, buck, rock, twitch. His face turned a shade of purple-red. Right before it looked like he'd pass out, Nisroc tapped Seskel.

"Nisroc," Seskel growled, his brown gaze latching on to Phe's. "Not with her. She's not part of this play."

Nisroc grunted.

"Come on," Seskel offered his hand to Nisroc, helping him up. "You can't help testing the boundaries, huh?"

Nisroc smiled grimly. "You didn't disappoint."

Seskel shook his head, as if disappointed. "If you messed up my progress with her, I'm going to beat you. Now, Oriana, is waiting."

Neither man looked at Phe as they left the room, their torsos speckled with red splotches.

"Willa, check on her," Seskel ordered right before he disappeared into his suite.

A shadow and swooshing noise had Phe spinning toward the banister.

The hawk landed, tucking its wings in as it walked the rail closer to her. Its predatory gaze fixed on her. It was magnificent. They stared at each other silently for a moment, one beast to another. Then it took flight, the wind from its wings rustling her hair.

Stars, that was odd.

"Get up," Willa demanded, looming over her with a cold glint in her eyes and a half-smile.

Phe used the chair to stand, an idea forming within enveloping guilt.

If I can't help Oriana, I'll help the next one in need.

13

Getting the sleeping tonic into Willa had been decidedly difficult.

There'd been logistical issues Phe had to contend with. Such as how to get to the bottle without Willa noticing? What to slip the tonic into? When? How to do all this while the woman watched her as though she were a petty thief trying to steal any baubles she could get her hands on?

The old motto "where there is a will, there is a way" paired well with Phe's persistence and a smidge of vengeance. Willa's half-smile still sizzled her vision.

It had been a flick of her hand over Willa's tea.

A moment where Phe clung to the table for support, forcing her to lean over Willa's food.

When Phe was done, the woman had consumed a dose that could put down an enraged bull, so it didn't take long until Willa's soft snores filled the darkened room.

Phe'd padded onto the balcony, swung herself over the side, and climbed down a vertical trestle filled with viny flowers. The note she'd written—*they're hidden in caves. Dr. Jorma? Auction tomorrow night, unknown where. All hands on deck. Ihrone to be beheaded at gathering*—burned in her bandeau.

Pulling her shadows to her, she carefully left the mansion and gardens behind. She hadn't meant to run, but once she was past the outer buildings, she found herself flying through the forest—trying to burn the guilt in her veins, one quick breath at a time.

It wasn't until sweat poured down her face, her thighs pulsed with blood, and the tight feeling in her chest deadened that she stopped. Brushing her sweat off her forehead, she took stock.

She was in the middle of nowhere.

There was a telltale thrum in the air and in her belly. The beginning signs of Drykz Forest calling her. Hands on hips, she circled backward, quickly. If the forest got a grip into her, she'd be compelled to go to it, and she didn't have time.

She retraced her steps back, all the while considering what she was going to do first. More than anything, she wanted to release the foal. She knew she was being irrational to set the foal's well-being above searching for the caves, especially since there was a likelihood she was already dead. Yet, something in her urged her to tend to the horse first.

Phe spotted a clearing next to a running stream: the perfect little spot to bring the foal. It was decided then.

She was certain General Bastion wouldn't be pleased with her decision and she'd hear no end to it. Then again, if she lived her life trying to please that man, she'd die a failure . . . or, her death would please him. Either way, she'd deal with his wrath when this was over, and she would never agree to a mission like this again. Having to stay in her Lady Orphne persona while in danger was beyond triggering and intolerable. It was debasing and disempowering and eye opening. It highlighted how ill-fitting her Lady Orphne persona—the persona she lived her daily Oceanid life in —felt.

Phe spent the next hour stealing supplies she could carry and carting it to the spot.

When she returned to the dilapidated shed, she ventured first to the rock she'd left her last update under. The rough stone was cold to touch when she tilted it. Her previous note was gone, and disappointment shot through her that whoever had taken it hadn't bothered to leave her an update.

With a sigh, she tugged her now soggy note free, hoping the ink hadn't gotten affected, and placed it in the barren spot. She should've expected General Bastion wouldn't have updated her. He left her in the dark so much, it was one of her and Kyra's running jokes about his bastardom.

Having accomplished that, she took a moment to take in the shed.

Heavy moss had crawled up the siding long ago. The roof sagged with years of neglect. The door she left cracked gleamed bright, new in comparison to the rest of the shed.

Maybe she'd burn it when this was all over.

Creeping through the overgrown meadow, she stopped to rest her hand on the door—its wood grain was rough, with several spikey ends poking her palm. She dropped the piece of rope to her feet, smelling the foulness from where she stood.

Please be alive, she implored, steeling herself.

Slipping into the dark void, into the wretched scent, she cooed, "Hey, baby."

The rattle of chains greeted her, followed by a low rumble, and Phe's heart unclenched.

"You're probably not going to like what I have planned," Phe shared, turning to stare in the direction she'd heard the foal. Her eyes had still not adjusted to the darkness. "I'm breaking you out."

The foal huffed.

Phe twisted and gripped the edge of the door she'd come in on— having pulled the hinges out the first night—and hefted the door to the side. Even though there was no one nearby, she controlled its descent. The less noise she made, the better. Once she'd discarded the door into the field, she grabbed the rope and reentered the shed.

Phe swatted dismissively at a few pesky flies as she crept to the foal's corner. This next bit was more challenging. She created a noose with the grainy rope, one that would slip over the horse's neck and tighten so that she could lead her away once she got the metal collar off.

"This is what's going to happen," Phe said softly, squinting at the foal's form. The foal was standing, which was a good sign considering how Phe had found her the day prior. "I am going to slip this rope," the rope hung in a malformed circle, "over your head and secure it."

The foal's eyes flared that weird red glimmer.

Adrenaline zinged into Phe's limbs, making her fingers tingle and her heart race. Ignoring the sensation, Phe continued. "I'll take off that metal collar and then we're going to walk out of here and to a spot near a stream where I've left you lots of food. Then I'll take the rope off and set you free."

The foal's ear twitched.

Why did Phe have a feeling this wasn't going to be easy?

Getting down to her knees, she slid forward, millimeter by millimeter, in the soft wet piles of feces, hands outstretched. "I don't want to hurt you. All I'm going to do is put this over your head."

The foal's eyes widened further than Phe thought was possible, flashing white at her. It squared off with Phe, ears stiff, and a front hoof stamped the earth once, twice, three times—the chain rattling.

"Please don't be scared," Phe cooed without moving her lips, unwilling to host a muck-covered insect in her mouth. Her wool tights were soaked through, and the buzz of what sounded like a swarm of flies engulfed her.

The foal shrieked, front muscles tensing.

"I get it. I get it. I'd be the same way, but I am not leaving you here another night. So, this has to happen."

The horse lunged at her. Phe bowed backward, rolling to the side, out of the way of the foal's hooves. Yet the foal somehow made a glancing blow to her shoulder.

"Huh," Phe retreated, her shoulder stinging. Switching her position from kneeling—which had been a hopeful approach—to squatting, she said, "First off, how are you even capable of fighting right now? I saw your flank yesterday. It was a mess. Second, you have some speed there."

The foal shriek-growled.

"Third, I'm impressed, girl. If I could keep you, you could be my war steed." Now Phe was talking nonsense. She was positive once she set this critter free, the foal wouldn't hang around to be found again. Then there was all the logistics of her keeping and training a war horse, General Bastion being the first major barrier. Yet the idea shifted something in the dark cove of her heart. Was that why she kept trying to name the foal?

The foal's gaze emitted its unwavering fierceness. She may be beaten and chained and severely malnourished, but she was not giving up.

Phe inched forward again, hating that she was going to have to do this the hard way. She wrapped the rope around her right hand and faced off with the fierce little thing. "If I had all the time in the world, I'd do this so differently. But I have to search this property for caves because you're not the only one who needs rescuing."

Phe was within its striking range, and the foal shrieked again.

Phe and the foal lurched at the same time. Phe shifted to the side, her right hand shoving the horse's neck away from her, and she grabbed onto the collar.

The foal immediately reared, hooves flailing, and got her in the ribs.

She muffled her OOOF from the impact, surprised at the creature's strength, and drove her body into the horse's side getting an awkward grip on the collar while sliding her elbow up the foal's neck to keep from being bit. The foal struggled, wrenching Phe about, as her piercing shrieks filled the shed.

All the while, Phe kept repeating, "I'm sorry, I'm sorry, I'm sorry."

Thank the seas Seskel didn't post guards anywhere near here.

Phe clung to the animal like a barnacle to a ship, riding out the waves of adrenaline this little creature had. The foal clipped her a few more times, and she knew she'd have bruises tomorrow. After what felt like an absurd amount of time, the horse lost steam, but not before the foal ruptured all her wounds and coated them both in blood.

"This is not how I wanted to do this," Phe said, unwrapping the rope from her right hand awkwardly. "I'm going to put this around your neck." Phe shifted to press the weight of her hips into the foal's body, then curved her body over the foal's, pinning her head to the wall. After a few attempts, she slowly worked the rope around the horse's neck.

Once that was complete, she awkwardly wrestled the lock-picking device from her amulet, keeping the foal pinned. The foal tried escaping again and Phe had to wait until she'd exhausted herself before she could start on the collar.

Finally, the metal collar dropped to the floor with a muffled thud.

Phe grabbed the loose end of the rope and retreated as quickly as possible into the corner farthest from the wide-open door.

The foal tracked her movements, using the wall for support, the wreck of her ribcage heaving.

"I think you are quite the fighter. If you weren't hurt and starved and a baby, who knows what would have happened?" she told the foal proudly, ignoring the throbbing parts of her from their tussle.

Something in Phe's gut twisted suddenly; she needed to return to the mansion. Phe scrunched her face. "I had plans to walk you all the way to the spot I found for you, but my gut is telling me I don't have time. So, I don't care if I have to carry you out of here, we have to go." She tugged on the rope and walked toward the door, beseeching the stars to help her.

The rope went taut.

If the foal could've attached herself to the wall, she would have.

Phe stepped into the field, sucking in the clean air, and moved to the side—to give the horse the impression she'd left—and waited. Minutes built up, one after another, without the foal moving.

Her stomach was now screaming that she needed to hurry, causing a cold sweat to break out in her armpits.

With a defeated breath, Phe silenced the cricket song. "Okay, I really, really didn't want to do this, but . . . seems that I don't have much choice." Phe stepped into the doorway, the foal's red glimmering eyes accosting her. This time, Phe's body didn't shudder. "We'll do it the hard way."

And the little foal showed Phe all of her fierceness, all over again —but it wasn't enough to stop Phe from picking her up and carrying her out.

14

Phe had just finished combing azalea oil in her hair—freshly showered after releasing the foal—and turned on the sink when the door to the bathroom flew open. Her shoulders stretched for the sky and her spine curved toward the sink as she shrunk into herself, pulling Lady Orphne to the surface.

Seskel loomed in the door's space, shirtless, pant button undone, and barefooted.

The smallest wave of assurance flowed through her that she'd had the forethought to discard her clothes outside and risk a quick rinse off, only to be replaced by a tsunami of apprehension so strong she broke out in gooseflesh.

The light blue silk robe she wore, and the slip of a nightgown beneath it, did little to hide her, hugging every curve. Her pulse pounded. She was practically naked.

Their eyes connected in the mirror. She read the flicker of relief crossing his features. Then he tore his gaze from hers and explored her body. A twinkle appeared in his gaze as he prowled to her.

Seas. Phe blinked and lowered her gaze. Her hands trembled as she turned the water faucet off and turned to face him, crossing her arms.

Seskel's teeth dragged across his lower lip suggestively and he stopped a foot from her, eyes roaming greedily. His eyebrows dipped strongly, and confused wrinkles rippled to life on his forehead. "Your legs."

Phe followed his stare, landing on the blooming bruises from the foal.

"I'll beat him." Seskel's lips compressed into grim unhappiness. He raised a finger, trailing it over her chest, his breath increasing. His fingers curled under the fabric that crisscrossed above her breasts.

Phe held her breath. A burst of fresh agony rippled under her skin, sending jolts of pain through her. The hair on her nape rose and her fingers tingled. If he tried to rape her, she'd let warrior Phe out.

Seskel closed his eyes, his fingers halting, and his nostrils flared. Then he reached his hand into Phe's hair, while the other pulled their bodies flush. He pressed his hard length into her belly. Lips on her earlobe, he said, "Cripes, I want to take you now, so bad."

Phe stiffened, forcing herself to take sips of air.

His hand slipped from her waist to her bottom, cupping it and bringing her closer, while he rubbed his chin on her neck. He ground against her, his teeth scraping over the thin material of her shoulder. She wondered what would cross that invisible line she'd decided on. How far would she let him go before she defended herself?

"Hey," Nisroc called from the other room. "Where'd you go?"

Seskel's head shot up, and he released her. His gaze searched her face for a moment, his chin firming into a tense line.

"I don't think I've ever seen Willa sleep so deeply," Nisroc stated dryly, leaning in the doorway.

Seskel turned, pointing to Phe's legs. "Look at what you did."

"Hm." Nisroc's stare roamed her scantily clad body, coating her in filth, and stopped at the bruises. A hand went to his chin and his brows raised.

"I told you she's fragile." Grabbing her wrist, Seskel stepped in front of her and tugged her forward.

"I see."

In the doorway, Seskel went chest to chest with the other man, and Phe shrunk down a little more, staying behind him. Her heart beating so loudly, she was sure they would hear it. "That's all you have to say?"

"Yeah." Nisroc shrugged a single shoulder then cocked an eyebrow. "Looks like I interrupted you. Why don't you pick up where you left off? I can watch, or . . ."

Seskel shook his head. "You're relentless."

"It's one of my best qualities." Nisroc smiled, the dim lighting deepened the sinisterness it held.

Seskel's laugh sounded like he agreed. "I'll meet you in the playroom."

"If you say so." Nisroc winked. Then he detached himself from the wall and strode off.

Seskel guided her to the bed and helped her in, robe and all. When he was done, he lingered over her, gaze fixed on her. Phe stared over his shoulder, body tense and ready. It looked as if he wanted to say something, do something, but after a moment, he left.

Phe rolled onto her side and curled into herself. She counted her inhales and exhales. Her skin was on fire, remembering his unwanted touch.

Gads, how am I going to survive the next two days?

15

Seskel bellowed a laugh. It was buoyant and carefree and filled the sizable room they were in. Chatter floated toward them from the dwindling groups of people—people who came to bid on the lives and flesh of others—dispersing into the night. The auction was complete.

Phe could barely contain the fury running in her veins.

They'd auctioned people.

Men.

Women.

Children.

Phe swallowed, yearning to break free from her Lady Orphne persona and become the thing of nightmares. Show these people what it felt like to be trapped, helpless, terrified, and knowing there was no chance they'd come out alive. She kept reminding herself these people would get what they deserved—that General Bastion would see to that. The reminder did nothing to quell her smoldering anger.

The leather mask covering Phe from head to the top of her chest, was suction tight, hot, and itched. *Gads, does it itch.* Willa had secured the straps—which she'd viewed as an opportunity to crush Phe's skull—adding to her throbbing headache. A headache that had been with her from the start of this blasted day.

The final piece to this torturous mask was the leash. There were two hooks at the base of her neck, and one on each shoulder, to which Seskel had secured a matching leash.

A leash.

Phe shifted away from Seskel—she'd been pinned to his side from thigh to shoulder all night. The proprietary hand at her lower back tensed, and the leash he held tightened, stopping her movement. A fresh burst of searing pain jolted her.

Phe resumed counting her breath. The pressure in her chest wasn't relenting, nor was her burning fury, but her breaths kept the blinding rage just enough in the shadows that she could continue the charade.

And, if Phe were to look for silver linings, the mask was a gift. Without it, Phe would've had to school her expression, and she wasn't sure she could've done that once they'd brought out the first child.

Thinking of children, her mind flitted to the little foal. She'd gotten the creature—with a lot of sweat and effort—out of that shed and past the neglected pasture. That's where her guilt started, though. Instead of leading the foal to the stream and what she'd prepared, she'd wrangled the foal free of the rope and watched her limp-run into the woods. Now, she worried. Did she do the right thing? Did she put the foal in more danger? Had a pack of coyotes killed her? Should she have waited until the mission was over?

If her emotions hadn't been so high . . .

A calloused hand touched her elbow and then traveled lightly over her bicep, stirring swirls of scorching pain so intense her whole body went rigid. Nisroc let his fingers rest there as he smiled at Seskel.

"It's a good night," Nisroc commented.

Phe leaned into Seskel, tucking her arm closer in an attempt to dislodge Nisroc.

Seskel's hardened stare fixated on Nisroc's hand.

Nisroc winked at Seskel, a smirk curving the corners of his

mouth. He appeared completely unabashed. "It's just so much fun to poke at you."

Phe pulled her arm free, curled it into her chest and then half turned to curve her body into Seskel's.

Seskel slid his arm around her and tucked her even closer to him, giving Nisroc a *keep-it-up-and-see-what-I-do* look. Which made feeling as though her whole body was one raw, exposed wound worth it if she was driving a division between them.

Nisroc's smirk drained into a frown, and he glanced around to make sure they were alone before saying, "Honestly, I'm still shocked you brought her."

"I am not worried about it," Seskel said, a finger tracing circles on her hip. "I like how you set up the space for this auction."

"I thought the raised dais was a good touch. Helped our guests to clearly see what they were bidding on." Nisroc skimmed the room, as if cataloguing the differences between Seskel's mansion and his old-style monolithic house.

Nisroc didn't live in opulence, but he lived well. Three stories well, four if Phe included the basement. The moderately-sized ballroom they had been relegated to most of the evening showed signs of his growing wealth. Chandeliers of sparkling crystals cast light. Though the curtains were drawn tight, the woodwork on the windows had embellished curves and glinted a brilliant gold color.

"And there were no incidents," Seskel commented, "which is always good."

Nisroc shoved his hands in his pockets. "I gifted my closest neighbors with a short holiday, just in case, and I had the trestle reinforced so if there were any issues, it'd be harder to see."

"Good. I like this new system. Bringing them in through the servant's entrance in those barrels seems more failsafe," Seskel said, the grip of his arm relaxing. "How'd we do?"

Phe gradually shifted away from Seskel's body, *One more night.* She just had to manage one more night until she'd give General Bastion the list of every single person who'd attended this auction.

"It was a lucrative night." Nisroc scanned the waning crowd. "Our guests were extremely generous."

"What I think," Seskel said, and Phe watched his gaze follow Nisroc's, "is that our clients have developed a taste, and we are the only source in all of Xafara that can fulfill their need."

Nisroc's gaze connected with Seskel's again. "I believe it also speaks volumes about their trust in our organization."

"Speaking of trust," lines of tension smothered Seskel's dimples, "have you gotten a full report on what happened with the monster? What are the guards reporting?"

"Well." Nisroc's head bobbed, and his face transformed into . . . was that unease? "The rumors were going crazy, and you know how superstitious people can be, so I pulled the detail off it."

"Did you pull the detail off before or after we acquired her?" The tone of Seskel's voice appeared calm and neutral, but none of it reached his eyes.

"Before," Nisroc admitted.

"So what you're telling me is a creature that has shown an array of unnatural abilities, that was somehow still alive after our experiments, was left unattended—"

"It was chained."

"And you didn't think I'd need to know." Seskel's severe glance would rival the most fearsome mother's. "Did you know I sent Orphne there as punishment, thinking there were at least four guards on hand if something went amiss?"

Nisroc said, "I didn't think the creature was something you concerned yourself with."

Seskel's unimpressed expression didn't change. "What do you know about its escape?"

"Very little. The beast was beaten three days ago. No one checked on it for forty hours or so and then they discovered the collar on the floor, still locked."

Phe's smile filled her chest. Yes, she'd done that. Gone back in, eradicated the evidence the foal had been fed and watered and locked the collar. It never hurt to play on people's fears, and Seskel's soldiers were scared of it.

"We should've killed it," Nisroc said.

Seskel laughed; it came out edgy. "You tried, remember?"

Nisroc drooped his shoulders. "I'm still trying to figure out what happened there. I swear, I beheaded it."

Bile churned Phe's belly, and she felt even worse for her manhandling of the foal.

"What I'm not impressed with is when you impulsively kill."

This time Nisroc's entire body donned a cloak of insincere apology. "I hadn't had time to visit the caves for relief..."

Phe's stomach clenched, and her gaze flicked between the two men, trying to read them. The two men had been together most of the day with Oriana, separating—it seemed—only to prepare for the auction. They hadn't mentioned an accidental death since Seskel insisted her joining him.

Oriana. Her heart slowed to a painful throb.

"Are you sure killing Oriana was accidental?" Seskel asked, sounding as though he didn't believe it.

The words knocked the wind out of her. Blood rushed into her ears until all she could hear for a cold moment was the roar of her heart.

She was too late.

Oriana would never reunite with her parents.

With a sheepish half smile, Nisroc said. "I was high strung and got carried away."

"I liked Oriana. I had plans for Oriana and Orphne." Seskel cracked his neck. There was an undercurrent between them, one that seemed to say, *I-think-you-did-it-out-of-spite.*

Phe agreed with Seskel.

A plethora of emotions swept Nisroc's face, remorse not one of them. "It's unfortunate she expired, but you have to say, it was quite magnificent the way she went."

Seskel shook his head, his expression unchanging.

They. Killed. Her.

Tortured her.

Stole her sunrise.

Because of me.

Because Lady Orphne is too weak.

Seas. I failed her. Phe's heart felt carved out her chest. At any point in this mission, she could've disregarded General Bastion's order and allowed assassin Phe free. Allowed herself to be powerful and capable and to actually have done something other than come up empty handed in her midnight sleuthing.

I could've saved her, but I didn't. I chose the mission over her. Breathing hurt. *I failed her.*

Unrepentant, Nisroc said, "I told you last night, we have a replacement in the caves."

A wave of heat flooded her, and her vision shifted. Literally shifted.

Don't kill them. Don't kill them. Don't . . . kill them.

Phe dragged her gaze to the ground and fought with her emerging warrior Phe. Fought the clenched fists pressing into her sheathless thighs. Her skin felt afire, though not from pain this time. This time she wanted—needed—to act. To lose herself in vengeance. Digging her nails into her palms, she forced her Lady Orphne persona forward. Breathing fumes, Phe reminded herself that General Bastion would ensure these men were punished, the right way.

Seskel scanned the now almost empty room. "I think we'll go there now. You coming?"

"What an excellent idea!" Nisroc smiled delightedly. "We have to celebrate tonight's success and," he pinned Phe with a pointed stare, "show her how lucky she is."

Within minutes, Seskel whisked Phe into his carriage, sat her beside him, and toyed with her hair. Nisroc planted himself across from her, his knee brushing against Phe's as they rode.

Phe sat ramrod straight, tension radiating from her, and rolled a braid on her amulet around and around and around. *One more day.*

Oriana's face flashed in her vision. Her whispered "I'm going to die in here" resounded through Phe.

Don't think about her. Phe cleared her mind of everything, shoved the caldron of her boiling emotions into a corner and drew upon Grum's engrained voice—*You worthless, useless piece of*—using echoes of the origins of her Lady Orphne persona to self-flagellate.

The carriage pulled to a stop at Seabreak Orphanage.

It was a behemoth building built on a bluff, surrounded by a sixteen-foot stone wall, built hundreds of years ago, before Kyra's family took oaths to protect Xafara, as a fort. Over the years, it had transitioned into many things: a monastery, a school, a marketplace. Yet for the last twenty-two years, it was an orphanage.

The orphanage General Bastion had tried to send Phe to eight years ago.

The orphanage she and Kyra supported, worked with, and visited often.

The orphanage Nisroc had grown up in.

The orphanage Dr. Jorma oversaw.

Seskel guided her out of the carriage, and the chill, crisp sea air whipped at her face as their party rushed inside.

"Mr. Brevil. Nisroc," Janteen, the headmistress, greeted them. "How are you?" Janteen's tone was soft and welcoming and very familiar to Phe.

How could you? Phe silently asked Janteen—whom she'd known for eight years. How could she act sweet and caring—the perfect guardian? How could you grow up an orphan—in this orphanage— and do this to those under your care?

Phe swallowed the how's, knowing intimately from her own Lady Orphne-warrior Phe experience, that people wear many masks.

"Janteen," Seskel responded with the same warmth, leaning in to peck her cheek. "I'm well."

"Hello, Jan, it's been so long," Nisroc said dryly.

Janteen eyed Phe, while gesturing for them to walk. "Are you going to introduce me to your companion?"

Phe snapped her gaze to Seskel.

Seskel shook his head and pressed her into his side. "She's here to realize how much I've spared her."

"Understood."

It was late. The children, who normally filled the hallways with laughter and infectious energy, sleeping. The hallways were lit with dim yellow lights and overcast. Huge pieces of old tapestry lined the walls to help with the heating.

Rumors of these hallways being haunted surfaced—not haunted like the secret passageways of House Nereid, where invisible things attacked with deadly force—but of cries through the night. Voices begging to be helped. Stories of women and children and men running down the halls, vanishing. The children with whom Kyra and Phe would speak would whisper fearful tales of those hauntings. Then, there were the children, with haunted eyes.

Phe's heart went off kilter.

Phe almost stopped.

Seskel and Nisroc and Janteen had grown up together, of sorts, at this orphanage.

How long had this been going on?

Seskel's comment, about seeing Phe that first time and wanting her since . . . did it mean this has been happening for at least eight years?

They entered the mammoth kitchen and then proceeded down a flight of stairs into the cellar. At a wine rack, Janteen opened a hidden door. A gush of stale, filthy air slapped Phe's senses. But that wasn't what stopped her.

It was the *feel* of the air.

It made Phe think of the stories she'd read of the death camps on the border of Aglizan and Shalexum. Those camps had begun as prisoner of war camps and, through negligence and human depravity, had evolved. Those who'd toured the vacant sidewalks, roads, and buildings, spoke of this heavy somber feeling. A weight in the air.

Some described it as grief.

A feeling of doom and dread.

A void of nothingness.

A sense of hopelessness would well in the chests, and unbidden tears would stream.

As if what occurred there—the horror, despair, grief, and depravities—haunted not just the soil, but the air you breathed.

The gaping blackness in front of her emitted all of that and more. The weight of all those emotions stampeded into Phe. Her chest tightened and her throat closed as Seskel guided her down the stairs and into the abyss they called the caves.

16

A shudder racked Phe, vibrating all the way to her bones, and she forced in a breath around the steel band of blazing pain caused by Seskel's arm at her waist. It didn't seem to matter they'd left the caves hours ago; the residue of whimpers and screams still echoed in her mind. An unwavering chill took residence in her body, unaffected by the mid-day heat, and what they'd done . . .

A wave of emotions—disgust, anguish, guilt, despair, revulsion—hit her, cording the muscles of her neck, locking her jaw, and causing her eyes to ache. At least, her stomach didn't threaten to revolt too, as it had the moment she'd walked into the gaping black void and down to the caves.

Those poor people.

The memory of a little boy, curled into the wall—

And like that, her stomach heaved, and she was gasping for breath.

She locked her gaze on the path ahead until Seskel's horse's head and ears faded. Focusing on how packed the dirt path was. How there were piles of fresh horse dung scattered on it. How green and clear the leaves bordering the path were. She focused on the fact that they were headed to the end of the organization, the end of this blasted, horrible mission, and that these men would never be able to hurt anyone again.

Seskel pulled her tighter against him, while his other hand—the one holding the reins—began to knead her thigh. In response, Phe reached forward and ran her fingers along the coarse coat of the horse's neck, to try to create distance between them. She could feel the bunching of the horse's muscles. Unbidden, the foal came to mind, and her heart lightened a smidgen. At least she'd released the feisty foal.

"Orphne," Nisroc said from beside them. Revulsion spiraled through her at the satisfied tone of his voice. "How do you feel?"

Spared. But she would never tell him that. Instead, she kept her gaze forward and flat and her mouth sealed.

When it became obvious she wasn't going to respond, Seskel did. "I think our point was proven and the metaphorical blindfold of what we are, what drives us, revealed to her has her petrified."

The coppery tang of blood burst into her mouth and she eased her teeth out of her cheek. If they believed that, then her role in this mission was a success.

'It's a good thing she sees us for what we are," Nisroc said, as if to reassure Seskel. "If she is going to be by your side, it's important she knows what she's dealing with and what the consequences of betrayal are."

At the mention of consequences, worry for Ihrone gripped her. Had General Bastion gotten her note?

Seskel shifted behind her, getting even closer—if that was possible—and touched his lips to her ear. "Curo's beheading is your fault."

Phe flinched from his touch, and he followed her, not letting up.

"He's dying because he hurt and touched you, besides Nisroc's grievance with him." He grazed his nose down the line of her neck, nipped at her shoulder, then up again. "Do you understand?"

"Yes, General," Phe muttered past clenched teeth and the stabbing pain in her head he caused.

"Let him be the lesson of what happens when someone touches what's mine."

"Does that mean you'll behead Nisroc too, General?" Phe whispered, her tone lathered in timidness and innocence.

Seskel laughed. "Nisroc is exempt from that type of punishment."

Phe glanced at Nisroc, who winked at her. Phe quickly averted her gaze.

The road ahead curved, and the two men fell into a preparatory silence. Once they cleared the bend, a small field appeared, parted by the road. On one side, horses were lined up. Some were tied to the perimeter tree line, while others had their lines staked into the field, with a few stragglers making their way across the expanse to the other side where a group of people stood mingling.

The chatter died as dozens of eyes settled on them.

Seskel and Nisroc steered their horses to the side of the small gathering of people. Phe scanned the sea of faces. She recognized Shadow Unit and the grasping greedies from the Final Swallow within the crowd. Beyond them, there was crudely made bench seating. The wood was old and discolored, with spots of green moss inching over the unclaimed territory. In front of the seating was a flattened area, which, at one point, had hosted a stage. The remnants of it were discarded in a jagged pile in the tree line.

The grass in this area was white with fresh growth, compared to the rest of the fields' long, green—now trampled—grass. In this area was another bench and a sturdy, two-foot tree stump.

Seskel reined his horse at the bench and, simultaneously, both men dismounted. Phe watched both of them broaden their shoulders, eyes scouring the audience in readiness to do . . . what, she wasn't sure. Seskel helped her disembark, then grabbed her forearm and walked her to the empty bench on the stage.

Phe sat, with her arms tight to her body, shoulders to her ears, upper spine curved into a C, and eyes downcast. Though, her heart was racing uncontrollably in her chest, both in anticipation and unease.

What if they don't know the plan to kill Ihrone?

The thought skewed her equilibrium, and warrior Phe punched at the barrier restraining her. There was no way warrior Phe would let Lady Orphne endanger anyone from Shadow Unit.

Seskel weaved his fingers into Phe's braided hair, positioning himself to stand over her at the end of the bench. Those fingers gripped her hair and wrenched her face to his. Pain lanced into her. His dark brown eyes radiated menace and frigidity.

Nisroc planted himself on Seskel's other side, one hand on his pommel, surveying their men.

All the gathered men and women sat in hushed tones. The weight of their gazes fell on Phe's bent head. Seskel gave her head a hard shake. "Uncover your amulet."

"Yes, General," Phe breathed, just loudly enough for him to hear, and pulled her sleeve to her elbow, exposing it. Kyra's distinct bracelet was unparalleled because of the singular, and striking, drop of water, the size of a large coin, hovering unnaturally in the center of the bracelet.

There were muffled exclamations.

Phe peeked through her lashes. In the row directly in front of her, Finian—a member of Shadow Unit—took up as much room as he possibly could. Legs splayed wide, he leaned deeply into Kirzia—another member of Shadow Unit—and had his arm over her shoulders. His brown eyes, which were often filled with mirth and mischievousness, were deadly hard and staring straight at her. Kirzia tilted her chin to Finian's ear, intimately close, whispered into it, then nuzzled the side of his head. The grimness melted from Finian's features, and he turned his head and captured Kirzia in a kiss.

Phe blinked and shifted her gaze, shocked. Rationally, she knew they were undercover, acting as a couple, but to see them passionately kiss in front of her felt wrong. Plus, out of all the team's members, these two were the ones often bickering the most. Mostly because Finian's superpower was to roguishly test everyone's patience, and Kirzia—at least with him—had the least of it.

The rest of the first row, Phe didn't recognize. Further into the seats, she spotted Orc's bald head, Roar's dull red, and Ihrone's cropped, tightly curled, wiry black hair.

"Gentlemen, I want to welcome you all," Seskel said, his tone cold. "What a pleasure this is to have us all gathered for the first time. As you all know, anonymity has been, and will continue to be, the foundation for our organization because it safeguards us. If one of us is apprehended and weak enough to talk, then the less you all know the better. But, there will be times, like today, where the messages we bring to you must be conveyed in person.

"We hope you've been able to meet the teams from other regions and get a better idea of how big we've grown. Last year, at this time, we had one the team, and our production lines were being established. Today we have five teams, one in each major city. We've established our clients, both within Xafara and on the mainland in tandem with a strong exporting crew, and last night's auction was a wild success. Well done."

Someone hooted, and applause broke out.

"We are here for a combination of reasons. With our rapid growth comes challenges, strategic and team-oriented, that we've not had to manage before. Thus, it is imperative now that our leadership take a more visible role. Let me introduce your leadership team." Seskel turned and indicated Nisroc. "Meet your colonel. If you would please rise when I call you. Captains Hukir and Nashka, and we have a promotion to this level that will be announced and celebrated toward the end. Lieutenants Jetts, Sarando, Raz, Brack, and Fade."

Phe was not surprised to see Fade was a petite female and Sarando an athletic one.

"Additionally, my contacts within Oceanid's guards have reported increased awareness of our presence and, with that, have placed more pressure on us. This is extremely problematic, and we've had some very close calls. Colonel, will you speak to our plans on this?"

Nisroc launched into a long speech on how the inventory would need to be moved in smaller batches and how the regions needed to find several storage units for their products that could maintain them for possibly a month or longer. He asked the crowd to think of solutions to manage any rumors and legal encounters, and to speak with him privately afterward. When he switched from this to discussing the current trends in their product, Phe stopped listening.

Impatience careened in her chest wildly. *When is General Bastion going to make his move?*

She could *feel* General Bastion's people watching. She closed her eyes, hoping to get a sense for where they were. They were close.

Seskel's grip tightened in her hair, as if to remind himself she was still in his grasp. "Now, we come to the celebratory part of our evening," Seskel proclaimed. "Let me introduce you to my lady, the one and only, Lady Orphne." Seskel yanked her by her hair to stand.

Pain seared through her scalp. Phe shot her gaze to Ihrone's. *It's-a-trap,* her gaze told him. Then she sought Roar, connecting with his blue gaze, because he had a knack for understanding her looks.

Roar's brow softened, subtly, and his responding glance seemed to say, *hang-in-there-its-almost-over.*

"I am sure you've all heard the rumors. Now, to be very clear with the rules on this, as I find myself particularly possessive of her: None of you will make eye contact or speak to her or touch her. If you do," Seskel sighed grimly, "the repercussions will be swift and brutal."

Seskel let this linger for a moment before continuing. "Lady Orphne is extremely fragile. Since I plan to grow old with her at my side, I will continue to need lookalikes." Seskel forced her head up, giving the crowd full view of her face. A fresh burst of pain flared in her head. "Take a good look, in case any of you were wondering what she looks like. Now, onto our celebratory news. Nisroc?"

Nisroc stepped forward, "Curo, Hukir, and Jetts, please join us."

Be careful. It's a trap. Be careful. Phe's heart pounded in her chest.

Nisroc toyed with his pommel absentmindedly while he watched them approach. When they were on stage, Nisroc beckoned for Curo —Ihrone—to stand next to him and clapped Ihrone on his arm, leaving his hand on Ihrone's bicep.

"Curo, why don't you tell us how you acquired Lady Orphne? We're all interested in hearing this."

Curo—Ihrone—launched into the story of how he'd followed her entourage to her treatment center and waited for an opportunity. When one was presented, which he described in detail, he grabbed her. He'd been worried about the dogs tracking them. His solution had been to have them both roll in feces to obscure their scents enough to escape their detection.

"I was wondering about that," Seskel stated, "because although he cleaned himself up, he did not clean up Lady Orphne. Placing her in the barrel in that state for . . ." Seskel paused, his tone hardened the more he spoke.

"Two days, General," Ihrone responded. Phe saw him make direct, unwavering eye contact with Seskel.

Seskel's sigh radiated his grimness.

Phe watched as Nisroc kicked out Ihrone's knee and forced him to the ground, calling out, "Now." Jetts, who stood on Ihrone's other side, joined in holding Ihrone in place, while Hukir took position at Ihrone's back.

Ihrone didn't struggle.

"You," Nisroc stated, and Phe assumed he locked gazes with someone. "I need the stump here." A man from the front row jumped to it, dragging the stump into position. When the man went to return to his seat, Nisroc barked, "Stay and hold him down."

Hukir sat on Ihrone's back and the new soldier took Nisroc's place.

Nisroc unsheathed his sword.

The field was held in taut silence.

"Curo, although correct in the assumption I wanted Lady Orphne, made grave errors in acquiring her. The first, he went rogue. To be extremely clear, he decided to abduct Lady Orphne, a well-known public figure, without authorization, and jeopardized our organization, our lives. We are still uncertain as to how this may fall, as there hasn't been any notification she is missing."

Seskel surveyed the crowd, and Phe had the distinct impression he was staring people down. "Rogue behavior in any way will not be tolerated. Everything you do is dictated by your leadership, and if you cross the line, you will find yourself with the same ending."

Phe flicked a glance to the tree lines. *What is General Bastion waiting for? Why aren't they breaking this up?*

"Next error, he hurt her. Left her breathing in feces for days. Her restraints cut into her, and she had no water or food."

She risked a glance at Finian and Kirzia. Finian had the gall to wink at her, but Kirzia's gaze was fixed on Ihrone, tense. She decided if Finian wasn't worried, she wouldn't be, but then remembered the amount of times he should've been worried but wasn't. She sought Roar's gaze, but this time, he wasn't looking at her, and his features were tense, too.

"His final error was to demand a promotion, and he was clear, if not agreed to, he would kill Lady Orphne."

Where is General Bastion? Phe's skin tingled, and something inside her seemed to press against her skin, as if wanting out.

"Positions within our organization are earned through trust and hard work. Blackmailing and any other means will only lead you here. Nisroc, ready?"

Acid swirled in her belly.

"Yes, General." The vile delight in Nisroc's voice had Phe straining at her control. *How is Ihrone so calm? What is General Bastion waiting for?*

Ihrone rolled his head to peer at her from the stump.

Nisroc gripped the hilt with both hands, widened his stance, and raised the sword overhead.

Phe's heart stuttered to a stop, and she unintentionally leaned forward—to do what, she wasn't sure yet.

"Oh, no, you don't," Seskel muttered and hauled her roughly back until all she could see was the tip of the blade. Then . . . with a whooshing sound, Nisroc brought the blade down.

Thump. Thump. Thump. Thump.

High seas! Phe's heart stopped.

Nisroc fell over, four quivering arrows embedded in his side, sword clattering to the ground.

Chaos broke loose.

Seskel and Nisroc's horses bolted. The other horses tied up began neighing, rearing, and bucking to get free.

People dropped to the ground, shuffling under the benches for cover.

More arrows streamed toward them. This time they hit the ground around the gathering, creating a circle—as if to say, stay in here.

A few brave and reckless souls sprinted for their horses.

A line of General Bastion's guardsmen bolted from the tree line.

The three people holding Ihrone were lumps on the ground. Ihrone stood in their place, a look on his face that said *I'm-going-to-make-you-wish-you-were-dead* as he stared at Seskel. It was an intense variation of a look Phe'd seen directed often at Finian.

Seskel swung Phe in front of him, yelling, "We've been betrayed! Fight! Kill him! Don't let them take you alive!"

The urge to wreck Seskel and then throw herself into the fray surged, her body becoming limber until her gaze clashed with Ihrone's and he shook his head no.

Flipping stars . . . Why isn't this over? She shoved warrior Phe, kicking and screaming, into her shadows and dredged up her Lady Orphne persona. She began shaking uncontrollably, fear thickening her throat.

The crowd lurched at Ihrone and General Bastion's guards. Seskel used the onslaught of fighting as a distraction, dragging Phe backward and into the woods. He let go of her hair to bruisingly grasp her arm and tow her alongside him.

Her Lady Orphne persona was quaking too much, her footing unsteady. She stumbled and dropped like a rock, glancing off the side of a spindly pine tree and into bushes. The suddenness of her fall almost toppled Seskel, too. Phe's breaths came in fast puffs, her corset strangling her lungs.

Seskel swiveled, tugging a knife free and shoving it in her face. "Get up, or I'll kill you."

Phe eyed the knife, grappling to get her quaking legs under her and working. If she were warrior Phe, relieving him of it would be easy, easier than catching her breath, and her body would be reacting a totally different way. Her heart ached as if betrayed by her Lady Orphne persona's unwillingness to release the reins to protect them. Her skin felt like it was stretching. The tingling had surpassed into a nasty itch. All she wanted to do was break from her Lady Orphne persona, yet Ihrone's headshake stayed her hand.

Gads, where the seas is everyone?

Stumbling to her feet, with Seskel's unrelenting grip, they ran deeper into the woods, Phe's breathing faster and more erratic and her footing clumsy. She fell again, forcing Seskel to stop again, and when he dragged her upright, she hunched over her thighs, her chest heaving against the constraints of her corset.

Seskel paced, his breathing controlled and steady, watching her. He stopped. "You were a trap, weren't you?"

Phe gulped air loudly, really, really not wanting to answer him. Warrior Phe tried to launch a new attack, trying to break free of the restraints Phe'd placed on her and her Lady Orphne persona could only tremble uncontrollably. Phe forced her words past tingling lips. "No-no, General."

Seskel prowled around her in a circle. "I don't believe you," then he sliced deeply into her bicep.

Phe hissed, and warrior Phe shot to the surface, shooting him an uncensored death glare.

Seskel snapped his head backward, startled.

Can't kill him. Can't hurt him. Phe gritted her teeth against the pain and wrangled warrior Phe down. She couldn't release her Lady Orphne persona. She shrunk into herself, her uninjured hand squeezing her injured arm right above the cut. Warm blood gushed, slipping into the spaces in between her fingers, into the fabric of her sleeves. *Hold on. It's almost over.*

Seskel slashed again. This time from her ear through her cheek, stopping midway through her upper lip. "You lie!"

Tears sprung to Phe's eyes from the pain, and she abandoned her arm to hold her lip in place. *Seas, this was the worst idea ever.*

"I see you're playing my favorite game," General Bastion stated as he reached them. General Bastion's pale scar, which ran from hairline to mid-cheek, was taut. That meant he was in one of his moods, and those were generally never good for her.

Phe's heart sank. *Why couldn't it have been someone else? Anyone else?*

Seskel lunged at her from behind, jabbing his cold, sharp knife point into her neck and wrapping an arm around her waist. He pinned her to his chest and dragged her back a step, "I'll kill her."

Mother of seas. Phe gave General Bastion a *what-the-heck-are-you-waiting-for* glower, her lip and cheek pulsing in agony with the movement.

"We can do that." General Bastion flipped a knife in the air in small, tight flips, catching its hilt. "But why don't we play a little game of pin the donkey, first, yeah?"

Before he was even done speaking, a knife was jutting out of her thigh.

Phe sucked in a painfilled breath. Her Lady Orphne persona collapsed, held up by Seskel's grasp at her waist. The knife at her throat sliced her.

"What are you doing?" Alarm spiked Seskel's voice. His grip on her tightened.

Another knife buried in the same thigh. "I hate when people interrupt me, and I interrupted you, yes? Weren't you in the middle of hurting her? I see no reason you should stop now that I'm here."

Phe pierced General Bastion with a glare that packed just how much she despised him. The bastard ignored her.

"Nooo." Seskel drew out the word, horrified with the realization he'd be blamed for this. Then he muttered into her hair, "Is he the reason you're scared of cages?"

Out of all the things he could say, why that? Phe almost—almost—allowed warrior Phe to yank a knife from her thigh and stab him. Handing any piece of information about her to General Bastion, especially her fears, was bad. This meant she would face those same fears over and over again in a perpetual cycle until the bastard was satisfied they wouldn't inhibit her ability to perform.

Three more knives joined the company of the others. General Bastion was neatly lining the knives vertically in her outer thigh.

"Hm," General Bastion's interest piqued. "Lady Orphne, I didn't know you have a fear of cages." The promise he was about to unleash endless torturous rounds of imprisonment did not go unnoticed by Phe.

Seskel retreated so quickly, Phe fell backward. "You're going to claim I did this."

Phe forced herself to sit, hissing around the knives sinking further into her.

The bastard wasn't done with her yet. He strode over, completely ignored Seskel, and squatted in front of Phe. He gave her a brittle smile.

Phe eyed the knife he languidly held.

"Why aren't you getting into this?" Bastion asked Seskel, deliberately sounding befuddled. "Oh, is it because there's nothing sexual in it? Should I . . .?" Bastion gripped the bodice of her dress and ripped it down the front, exposing her corset. *What is with people ripping my dress?* "Do this?"

Every molecule in Phe's body blared how much she loathed him.

All of a sudden, a blur came from behind her and slammed into Bastion, knocking him over. He shot to his feet, blood dripping from his face.

A four-legged body positioned herself over Phe's legs with a familiar growl-shriek-grumble.

Phe blinked, confused at the turn of events.

The foal's skeletal body, littered with wounds, stood tense and ready. Her ears pinned to her head, eyes wide, and Phe could hear her struggle to breathe.

General Bastion stood stock still, staring at the foal.

"Oh, bloody seas!" Seskel exclaimed, bolting away from them and disappearing into the trees.

"General Bastion." Phe stretched a hand toward him. "She's only trying to protect me."

Phe watched his eyes rove over the foal, knowing he didn't miss any details. In their silence, they could hear Seskel crashing through the woods and then there was a huge crack.

"Got him!" hollered Finian.

Whatever it was she saw change in Bastion's body or eyes drove Phe to her feet and she yanked the foal by her mane behind her. All the air was knocked from her, as a blade embedded into her stomach. She crumpled around the wound. *Oof!*

The foal shrieked again, fighting Phe's grip.

Enough is enough. With her good hand, she jerked the knife in her stomach out and volleyed it at him. The pleasant thud of its impact, which—admittedly, she was surprised she made—was satisfying.

A predatory smile bloomed on Bastion's face, promising retribution, as he pulled the blade from his thigh.

The forest behind her sounded as if it was being pulverized.

"Don't even think of hurting her," Phe seethed, her cut upper lip trembled weirdly when she talked, and her hold on the foal was slipping.

"Orc, you're needed. Lady Orphne is injured," Roar called, silently stepping into the clearing. Neither Bastion nor Phe broke their *I'm-going-to-kill-you* stare off.

"Yes, sir! Lady Orphne—" Orc, the unit medic, rushed toward her, only to stop when the foal wrenched herself free and inserted herself between Phe and everyone else.

Flinging her injured hand in a stop gesture and ignoring the explosion of pain it caused, Phe said, "Don't hurt her," through clenched teeth, still not tearing her gaze from Bastion. From her earliest memories, people had hurt her. Deliberately, cruelly, venge-fully hurt her, and no one in her memory had ever tried to protect her. Yet this mess of a foal, who'd valiantly tried to kill Phe herself at their last encounter, just did.

That was it. She was keeping the feisty little thing.

"What is . . ." Orc let his question trail off, shifting gears. "Ihrone. Some help here with the horse?"

"On it," Ihrone said, calmly stepping in front of Orc and crouching eye-level with the foal.

Finian threw Seskel into the clearing. He landed heavily on his side, arms bound behind his back. He eck'd and scuffled away.

"Ph . . . Lady Orphne, what happened?" Finian exclaimed.

"I didn't do it!" Seskel proclaimed from his kneeling position. "General Bastion did."

A grimness rolled through Shadow Unit like a dark storm cloud, and they all ignored Seskel, talking at once over each other.

"Fin, your shirt," Orc instructed, holding his hand out expectantly.

"Kirzia, Finian, take him into custody," Roar commanded.

"Yes, sir," they chorused. Immediately, Kirzia hefted Seskel to his feet and Finian forcefully propelled him into the woods after tossing his shirt to Orc.

"Hey there, girl," Ihrone murmured soothingly, offering his hand to the foal. The foal flinched and stamped her foot. "We need to help the lady behind you. She's hurt pretty badly, and we want to help you too, if you'll let us."

The blood in Phe's veins chugged slowly, and a lightness crept into her head. Ihrone's words melted into the thrumming in her ears, but whatever he was saying worked. Tension in the foal's body eased.

"Phe, tell this little gal it's okay to trust us," Ihrone requested.

Intensifying her glare at General Bastion, she lowered her voice into soothing waters. "Baby, you can trust everyone but him." She tilted her chin toward Bastion, putting punch into the *but him.*

Ihrone stood and cautiously pulled a length of rope from a pocket. Moving slowly, he fashioned a lead and oh so carefully slipped it over the foal's head, announcing, "This little gal and I are going to trek back. We'll see you there."

Phe grunted, unwilling to break her stare off with the bastard to glower at the foal and Ihrone. How in the seas did Ihrone do that? The foal just let him put the lead on. No fight. While Phe—who'd fed her for a few days—was still bruised from the foal's rescue mission.

Orc inched warily around the horse while ripping Finian's shirt into strips. He squatted at Phe's side; gaze fastened onto the cut on her arm. Phe carefully maneuvered her elbow on her injured arm, giving him space to slip in a tourniquet. Wordlessly, he did, staunching the flow.

As the foal passed General Bastion, she slowed and rumbled threateningly. Ihrone didn't pause a beat, hustling her past as if she hadn't threatened someone like a dog.

Roar strolled in between Bastion and Phe. "General, everyone's rounded up."

"Permission to be myself?" Phe asked.

A muscle ticked in General Bastion's cheek, "Granted."

On her inhale, warrior Phe surged to the surface, shoving her Lady Orphne persona aside. Gritting her teeth, the searing, all-consuming pain—settled into the space of experienced tolerability. The tightness of her lungs—expanded. The trembling in her core—her heart—quieted, replaced by a calm determination.

Pressing a hand across her face to hold her lip steady, Phe said. "There are others who are part of the organization who are not here. Have you arrested them?"

Orc jostled her as he tied off her thigh tourniquet, leaving the knives there in place. Then he stared at her eyes, his brow furrowing a tad. "Did he hit you in the head? Can you see how many fingers I'm holding?"

He held three fingers up.

Without pulling her gaze from the bastard, Phe muttered, "Three."

"Phe, let me see." Orc's hazel gaze scoured her face, and he gently tugged at her hand. Phe carefully released the pressure, inhaling deeply as she absorbed a rush of pain and switched her attention to Orc. She watched Orc examine the wound, his face calm and expressionless, then met his green streaked hazel eyes. "It's a good thing you don't scar."

Phe's chin dipped in agreement; seriousness pinched the corner of her eyes. "It's a good thing I heal quickly."

Orc quirked one side of his mouth up. "And that you can take a beating and keep on ticking."

Her throat swelled with remembrance of the last seven days,

threatening to choke her. Clearing it, she flicked her gaze to General Bastion, who limped toward them. He had crafted his own tourniquet.

Roar joined and squatted at her side, his blue eyes capturing hers. "What can you tell us?"

"Were you able to trail me to Nisroc Aldes's house last night?" Phe asked, unsure if her notes had been received.

"Yes. General Bastion sent out crews that swiftly and quietly apprehended everyone involved," Roar said.

"The people from the auction are safe?" Relief flooded into her and made her limbs feel feather light. "Thank the seas. We should compare lists to ensure you got everyone."

Roar nodded. "We will."

"Sorry, Phe, gonna have to carry you, there's no way you can walk out of here *without* hurting yourself further," Orc interrupted apologetically, then quickly tacked on for good measure. "And there are a lot of people milling about."

Phe grunted. She couldn't argue with that.

"Phe, I'm going to lift you now," Orc said while sliding his arms under her. He stood, cradling her to his chest as if she were a newborn kitten.

Phe hissed long and hard, fisting her hands. *Seas, that hurts.*

Orc didn't wait for her to get a handle on her pain before striding away.

General Bastion, who was striding next to them, waited until her hiss fizzled out before saying, "We were not able to track you after the auction. Did you learn anything else?"

Grappling with breathing, she didn't respond right away. When her lungs finally relented from their boycott, she said, "Did you know Seabreak Orphanage has a dungeon?"

She waited, giving Bastion and his endless memory time to recall it.

He released a sigh that sounded frustrated. "I did."

"They're holding people there. The headmistress Janteen is involved. You know about Dr. Jorma. I'm sure many others are, too,"

Phe said. "And in case there are more dungeons than I know about, the entrance to this one is in the wine cellar. And you need to rescue Amaia from Seskel's estate. She's in his playroom, it's—" Orc made a movement that electrified her body, cutting her off.

No one spoke while she tussled with the pain.

Clearing her throat, she croaked, "Willa was coerced into keeping me there. Seskel threatened her and her family and friends lives if my presence was made known."

"How's your pain?" Orc's gaze dropped to her face for a moment.

"Fine," Phe muttered, ignoring the movement of Orc's disappointed sigh. She'd decided a long time ago, if she could talk, she was fine. Briefly, she wondered about how her Lady Orphne persona experienced the same pain.

"What happened to Oriana?" Roar asked.

"They killed her," Phe said in hollowed tones.

"Where's his playroom?" General Bastion demanded.

"In his private library, tilt toward you the book *Forbidden Pleasures*." As Bastion's speed increased, she called after him, "I don't know if there are other secret rooms." He didn't acknowledge her.

"Alright, Phe, is it okay if we go over the list? Or do you need a break?" Roar asked, shielding her and Orc from a tree branch.

Phe scoffed. She couldn't take a break when there were lives at risk. "Let's do this."

17

The pervasive chill of the caves burrowed into her bones, and the heaviness in the air wrapped her in its suffocating grasp. She rubbed her arms, trying to infuse warmth past the wet layers of her clothing and shake off the blanket of doom and dread and hopelessness and horror that permeated the space. It was a wasted effort.

She shouldn't be here.

General Bastion had explicitly forbidden it—citing that it was a crime scene and she'd somehow disturb it. It had been enough of a warning to hold her off from dragging her injured body from the safe house General Bastion had acquired for Shadow Unit and her to stay, where she could heal from her injuries and maintain the secrecy of her dual life, to the caves for the past five days. Knowing the caves were crawling with people investigating and cataloguing every nook had held her at bay, even at night. Then, she'd heard they'd removed the ancient torture devices and signaled this part of their investigation was over.

However, they'd left the lights—probably intending to walk people through the rough rooms, talking them through the crimes carried out here. The blazing lights were on when she'd descended, and a part of Phe wondered if it was their attempt to drive the shadows from the space, too.

Soundlessly, she padded toward the rear of the cave system, guilt chewing its way through her heart.

When she'd left the safe house, the weather had reflected her mood. Rolling thunder and heavy rains had accompanied her on her run, unsuccessful at washing away her failure.

People—not just Oriana—had died.

It had been over a week since Seskel and his crew were arrested, and the investigators had been making progressive arrests since. Those who'd been rescued were still being held by the Xafarian government, receiving care—both physical and emotional. From the survivors, the investigators discovered the majority hadn't been abducted, they'd been sold or coerced.

During the three years Phe'd spent with Grum, she'd seen it all. People had been forced or sold into slavery by partners, family members, friends, neighbors, gangs. The worst—she thought—were the parents who sold or traded their children. After those incidents, Phe was often left wondering if that's what her parents had done . . . even though Grum had boasted of finding her wandering in Tryst Forest.

A scuff sounded from the stone stairwell.

Phe's swiveled, waiting for the culprit to emerge.

"It's me," Roar announced.

Phe sighed and waited for him to catch up to her. He stopped over an arm's length away. "I didn't have a nightmare. Why are you following me?"

"I worry about you."

Phe grunted in response, accustomed to his response. She rolled the warm, rounded rock she had in her palm. She'd picked it up when she sensed him following.

"Why are you here?" Roar asked.

Phe cleared her throat, answering him by striding toward the back of the caves.

He matched her pace. "You came to see how they died?"

Phe's stomach tightened, and she tilted her chin defiantly.

"It wasn't your fault," Roar said.

This time, Phe huffed. "If I'd left Seskel that night and immediately reported this place ..."

"You wouldn't have found us."

"But—"

"Phe, there was nothing you could've done. Had you left that night, Seskel would have cancelled the team gathering. If he'd done that, General," a repulsive shiver seized Phe's shoulders at the word *general,* "Bastion wouldn't have been able to arrest the crews. In fact, you were the key to informing us about this location, and even though people died, those deaths are not on you."

Phe frowned with denial, her look silently saying *I-could-have-done-something-to-save-them.*

"You couldn't have anticipated General Bastion would arrest everyone who attended the auction. Or that a servant from one household would have overheard General Bastion's guards," another wave of revulsion tightened her shoulders, "and reported the arrest and intel to Janteen, who'd then barricade the doors and try to remove any evidence by killing everyone."

Phe scowled at Roar, and he continued unperturbed. "In my opinion, you were the key to us saving the lives we did."

Her chest burned as she recalled how the bastard had waited for as long as he had to interrupt Seskel's gathering. And how he'd chosen to hurt her in front of Seskel—which she was pretty sure had been to test her ability to stay in her Lady Orphne persona—instead of arresting him immediately and conferring with her. Because from the reports, they'd been minutes too late to save the six people Janteen and her crew had thrown off the cliff side.

Phe spotted the door cut out of the rock face. Its dark wood surface was muted, and centuries old rust coated the metal fixtures on it. She'd learned this doorway had been created when the fortress and the dungeon were built. The door opened to a small outcropping and then a sheer drop of hundreds of feet to the Bynd Sea below. It was used to execute and dispose of prisoners' bodies in one fell swoop and was the sole reason why they hadn't found any victims' bodies.

"What are you looking to accomplish?" Roar asked.

The latch was a heavy cast iron, rough and porous to the touch. Phe pulled it free, dropping her hand to grip the door handle. "I want to see what they saw before they were tossed to their deaths."

It wasn't a want; it was a need. A need to see what they saw. A need to imagine what it felt like to be pushed off the edge. A need to pay homage to those she'd failed.

Phe dragged the heavy door toward her. The hinges screamed, filling in Roar's silence. A gust of sea air slapped her immediately, clearing the filthy scent of the dungeon from her senses, and sprinkling her with rain.

She stepped onto the outcropping, its surface smooth from the years of use, the cool rain pelting her.

In front of her was emptiness.

A void she knew plummeted thousands of feet along the sheer cliff walls that made Xafara impregnable. A burst of lightning lit up the night sky, giving her a brief glimpse of where sky and sea met.

Her heart fluttered.

"Do you know why Seskel was called the . . ." She couldn't bring herself to say General.

Roar stood at her back in the doorway, close enough to touch. "It was a nickname given to him during his short stint in the military. When he created his organization, he recruited his friends from the military, making them his officers, so the name stuck."

"Ah." Phe closed her eyes and tilted her face. Rainwater streamed down her cheeks.

I'm sorry. She silently apologized to the stars—to Oriana and the others who'd lost their lives—and to those now looking down on her from their journey up the celestial stairway. *I'm so sorry I failed you.*

"Phe, their deaths aren't your fault," Roar repeated.

Thunder growled ominously, answering for her.

"General Bastion is going after every single person involved, from those who sold or coerced people to the organization to Seskel." His tone was reassuring, as if he needed to prove they were doing all they could. "He's even working with the Shalexum government to locate those who were smuggled and trafficked there—which we're surprised they've agreed to help with."

When she didn't say anything, he continued. "We have a bet going. Ihrone, Orc, and Kirzia believe Shalexum is helping because they know we'll track down any survivors with or without their permission. Finian and I agree, but we're betting this is the first rumblings of change for Shalexum's slavery laws. Aglizan and Piopina are applying a lot of pressure—they don't like their citizens being abducted either."

Gads, I hope that's true.

A gust of wind changed the direction of the rain. It started pooling in her ear. Phe had lived in Shalexum as Grum's slave until she was ten. She knew how engrained in the culture and beliefs slavery was and that it would be a hard, long fight.

"That would be a miracle," she said, wiping her face and opening her eyes.

Immediately, a series of massive lightning bolts showered the seascape. Hints of blue intertwined with brilliant white light, illuminating the tumultuous clouds and raging sea. Just like her mood.

"You want in on the bet?" Roar retreated into the cave, signaling to her to come back. Back from the edge. Back to them.

She turned to Roar. Shadow Unit bet on everything. It was a quirk of the unit and led to never-ending jokes and challenges. Sometimes Phe joined them, yet she couldn't bring herself to bet on this, not with how Shalexum's slavery had shaped and shaded her life.

"Not this time." She massaged her palm with the rock and peeked over her shoulder, catching a last glimpse of the view before Roar shut the door.

As they quietly left the fortress, Phe bundled her heart-wrenching guilt and sadness at failing Oriana and the others and funneled it into the rock.

It was a little thing she and Roar had come up with years ago, when she rarely spoke. Roar had suggested she take a rock and imagine filling it with her past or nightmares or fears or whatever sent her running in the middle of the night. Then she would offer her burden to Roar, who accepted the weight of it with no stories or explanations. No questions asked.

When they were outside the Orphanage in the pouring rain, Phe stopped and caught Roar's blue gaze, holding her fist out.

Before releasing the rock, she asked, "Did you know Oriana was named after the sunrise?"

"I didn't." Roar slid his hand below hers, and she dropped the rock into his palm. He rolled it between his palms, his blue gaze softening. "Seems fitting to honor her memory by name this mission, 'Operation Sunrise.'" He pocketed the rock. "For the sunrise we lost and for those we were able to save."

Yes. Her chest tightened and a wave of survivor's guilt washed over her.

The name 'Operation Sunrise' seemed perfect. It felt like a fitting tribute to the ones they'd lost and those they'd saved, but it also served as a reminder of the fragility of life. As she took a deep breath of salty air, water pouring down the contours of her face, Phe felt mixture of sadness and regret, wishing she'd been able to have done more—to have saved her. Yet, in a way, the name also gave Oriana a sense of immortality, an endless stream of sunrise that Phe would remember her by.

She grunted her agreement.

"Back to the safe house?"

"No, I have to check on Kyra." Phe wiped rainwater from her face, then cheekily asked, "Do you plan on following me to Kyra's, too?"

A smile curved Roar's lip, and he shrugged. "Maybe."

EPILOGUE

One Month Later

Phe's forearms rested on the rough wood beam of the fence, and she watched the foal bolt around the pasture, happily showing off and burning through all her energy. It was amazing what a month of proper diet and care had already done for her. She still wasn't out of the dark yet—in fact, she had many months of recovery to go until she'd be given the all-clear physically. Mentally, who knew how long it would take. That was a struggle Phe knew all too well.

The little thing zoomed by her, then stopped and backtracked to nuzzle Phe's arm. Her whiskers tickled Phe as she brazenly snuffed Phe in search of the carrot she smelled.

Phe's smile stretched the limits of her face, and her heart burst into a joyous song. Over the last four weeks, the foal had progressively gotten more and more comfortable with her—but it was only within the last few days she'd started to do this.

Playfully, Phe scrunched her face, giving the foal her empty hands to smell, careful to keep her elbows together. "Do you want more carrots, Eve?"

The foal's face withdrew, her eyes widened ridiculously, and an ear twitched. Phe watched in fascination at the foal's reaction—she clearly did not approve of the name—and wondered if she'd stay this time for the carrot or prance off in a fit. Something over Phe's shoulder caught the foal's attention, and her whole body stiffened. With a quick flick of her gaze to Phe, she was off.

Phe didn't need to look to know who approached her. It was the bastard.

She'd avoided him as much as possible, which was difficult considering he and all of Shadow Unit were staying in the same safe house as her on the outskirts of Oceanid. If Phe could help it—and she put a lot of energy into helping it—she was never alone with him. The bastard behaved better when there was an audience.

Truth was, they needed to talk. She'd officially requested to be sent to Kyra two weeks ago and hadn't heard a word.

It didn't mean Phe had to be polite about it, though.

So, when he settled a few feet from her, she refused to acknowledge him. She kept her attention on her little foal, who'd stopped about twenty feet away, stance wide, gaze suspicious, and ears perked. From her stance, Phe wasn't sure if the feist-ball would charge. She'd made it very clear she considered Bastion an unfriendly.

Bastion let the silence hang between them, as if he was warming the waters. Acclimating her to his presence. From Phe's peripheral, she saw his relaxed profile, which didn't relieve her tension.

"How is your recovery going?" he asked.

"Fine." Phe drew in a solacing breath then arched the brow he could see, telling him by the movement to get on with it.

"Your physical healing this round was impressive. Orc told me your wounds healed within four days, even though you limped for a bit after that. He also shared your distress at being touched has exponentially increased."

Again, Phe waited. There was truth to that, except with the foal. She had no physical reaction to her at all, but she wasn't going to tell him that.

"You're not sleeping, you've been disappearing on long runs, and your sparring is considerably more aggressive than normal." Phe rolled her eyes, anger flaring in the pit of her belly. She knew where this was going. "Her Grace reports that when you sneak in to visit her, you're quieter than usual and very reactive to touch. These are a few of the reasons why Her Grace and I discussed and declined your immediate return. We've decided to reevaluate in a month's time."

Phe slowly twisted to face him, letting him read the lines of aggravation in her body. Why they would deny her request to return to Oceanid officially blew her mind. She'd lived there, under social scrutiny and judgment, when she was ten times worse, twenty times worse, and they would deny her now?

When she visited Kyra tonight, they were having words.

"And then we have this foal." Bastion turned to meet her death glare head on, unintimidated. "She's young and needs a lot of care and attention and protection. If you were to return, who would do that?"

Phe quirked her head. "She'd come with me."

"No, she wouldn't."

Phe tsked, knowing Seskel and his group were the cause of this. What those fools reported about the foal had been hyped-up fantasy talk. She'd admit the little horse had nuances—like her mannerisms and her odd behaviors and her ability to heal, which only aligned Phe to the foal more. The foal reminded Phe of herself, and not just with the foal's unnaturally fast healing. It was their shared understanding of the pain and hardship that life had dealt them. When Phe looked at the foal, she saw something in her eyes that mirrored Phe's own determination and resilience, and it filled her with a sense of hope and connection that she had been missing for so long, and it made her very protective of the foal.

"We're watching her for any of the behaviors Seskel and his crew reported. Until I deem she is not a threat, she stays here," Bastion continued.

Phe clenched her jaw. Of course they'd watch the foal, just as they'd watched her when she'd first arrived. It was as if they'd all forgot, when someone has survived horrible circumstances, they don't come out of it unscathed—at least, not at first, when the wound is still open and raw and barely treated. And the foal was no exception.

The other day, Finian asked if the foal had been raised in a pack of feral hounds. He could've been asking because she growled, but then, it could have also been a number of other reasons, such as her reaction when they'd introduced her to the other stable horses. Suffice it to say, it didn't go well. Or the fact that she handpicked who cared for her, and when it wasn't one of them, chaos and destruction would follow . . .

Seas, the bastard is right.

"I concede to your point," Phe admitted, letting the anger seep from her. She wasn't returning to Oceanid without the foal, and at this point, the girl was a little too wild to bring to the orderly stables at House Nereid.

What if they put her in with Shadow Unit's horses? Those horses were not the docile stable horses the foal had met. They were battle-trained beasts that would have no problem putting the foal in her place and maybe teaching her some manners. She'd have to talk to the team about the idea.

Phe resettled on the fence and noted the foal had crept toward them stealthily. Phe stifled a smile; the foal was the cutest little thing, thinking it could sneak up on either of them. Phe's heart did a weird flip-jump. "Maybe we should train her to be a war horse?"

"The way I see it, we have two choices. Right now, she's too aggressive and dangerous. If she doesn't improve, she'll be put down." Phe tensed. They'd have to do that over her cooling, dead body. "If she improves, we'd be doing her a disservice to not battle train her."

Phe grunted.

With that, Bastion turned and started walking away.

"I have a few things to say," Phe said, staring at her foal and fidgeting with a braid on her amulet. A hawk soaring overhead caught her attention.

Bastion turned and waited.

"What you did was . . ." Emotion welled in Phe, smothering her voice for a moment. It wasn't that he hadn't filled her full of knives or arrows or beaten her senseless before. He'd done that and worse over the years in the name of training. But he'd never done it in front of people, and he'd never, never added sexual overtones to it. Plus, he often kept his crazy between just them. Sure, he treated her poorly in front of Shadow Unit, but he kept his behavior in line when they were together. He'd only ever tried to kill her when they were alone.

It was Bastion's turn to wait Phe out.

Phe drew in a fortifying breath, lifting her fingers to tick off his grievances. "You hurt me. All of which you did in front of Seskel—which I'm still not sure if that was a test to see if I could continue in the persona, or if you just wanted to shred my thigh for target practice—all while he had his han—" This time, it was her anger that choked her. "Hands on me."

The foal was getting suspiciously closer.

"Which . . ." Phe shoved her anger in a corner, knowing she didn't need to point out everything he'd done. He wouldn't apologize for it. She needed to tell him his actions were in poor form without giving him incentive to do it again. He hadn't brought up Seskel's cage comment, but she was no fool. She knew he was biding his time on that one. ". . . delayed me in giving you crucial information and resulted in unnecessary deaths."

"I was impressed with your ability to maintain the course," General Bastion stated, watching the foal. "And I regret that in testing you, there were causalities."

Phe side-eyed him. This conversation was surreal. Not only had he listened to her—which was a lengthy speech for her—he'd diplomatically answered her, too. "I will no longer call you by the title General." Because even thinking of the word General showered her in a sea of revulsion and made her want to vomit.

Bastion took a moment to chew this over, probably considering how much effort he wanted to exert in trying to beat her into submission over it. He sighed, most likely concluding that no matter what he did to her, she wouldn't submit. "I'll allow this."

Phe almost snorted, covering it in a half-cough. She hadn't been seeking his approval. "And I will never go undercover with my Lady Orphne persona again."

Bastion pressed away from the fence, his body telling her he was done with the conversation. "Hm, did you find her too stifling for you?"

Phe frowned at him.

He pinned her with a brief, pointed look before he turned and walked away. "Don't you think it's odd you're trying to rush right back into her?"

"No," Phe called. Anger flared in her belly again as she watched him leave. "I'm not rushing. I'm trying to do my *job*, which is to protect Kyra." Phe had fully turned, arms extended at her elbows, palms up. "Can't protect Kyra when I'm not with her, can I?"

The bastard gave her a quick, loaded glance that said, *you-keep-telling-yourself-that.*

Gads, she wanted to punch him.

Clenching her fists, she watched as Bastion crossed paths with Ihrone and Roar. They stopped to chat briefly. Phe watched until Roar's blue gaze found hers. He quickly scanned her—always making sure she wasn't hurt, as if she were clumsy. He gave her a tight smile.

Phe twisted and reached into her sleeve to pull out the carrot she'd hidden there, knowing the foal was about a foot from her, and smiled.

"Hey, Della, baby." Phe broke the carrot into three parts while the foal had the gall to look offended. Phe smirked, offering her the first portion of carrot. "Did you hear? We have some work to do on your manners."

The foal flicked both ears toward her rear, greedily chomping the carrot. Phe scanned her ribcage, still amazed the veterinarian had mended all her broken ribs. "Well, you can't travel with me if you don't allow others to care for you, and you have to get along with other horses and stop breaking things when you're mad. If you do that . . ." Phe's tone gradually inclined toward excitement.

The foal ignored her, too focused on mouthing Phe's fist and leaving a trail of drool all over her.

". . . We'll train you to be a war horse." The thought of the little foal as her war horse had Phe's heart doing somersaults. With the foal's temperament, the two would be near invincible—not that there was a war she'd be allowed to fight in, as her purpose was to be Kyra's secret weapon and that meant living as Lady Orphne when she wasn't training. She opened her palm, and the foal scarfed the carrot up. "But first we need a name."

"You're still trying to name her?" Roar said, sliding up next to Phe.

Phe shot him a glance. This was the closest he'd stood to her in a month, not that she was monitoring. He still hadn't touched her even though the mission had ended—and that was odd. Not that she wanted him to, necessarily, but she'd gotten used to his friendly touches; their absence felt *off,* as if something were wrong with their friendship. This made her wonder if maybe he was right when he'd harped about how touch can be healing over the years.

"Yea—" The foal stuck her face into Phe's, cutting her off. "Ooof. I've gone through at least a hundred names." Phe snuggled her face into the foal's bony one and rubbed her neck. She drew out the moment because she knew the girl was searching for the last piece of carrot.

"What about Sam?" he offered.

The foal snorted disdainfully at him.

"Tried that already." Phe narrowed her eyes at the foal, puckering her lips in playful thought at her. "Edva?"

The foal's eyes lit up.

"I think we got a winner," Roar said, his tone filled with warmth.

"Aww, Edva." Phe gave her the last carrot, a giddy warmth spreading across her chest. Even though it was just a name, it felt like more . . . as if naming Edva was the final piece to solidifying their relationship, it was the beginning of a whole new chapter, and it ended chapters, too. Edva would never be abused again, and Phe—it felt like—would have a consistent companion who, no matter if she was warrior Phe or Lady Orphne, would travel with her. A sense of love and belonging, one she was wholly unaccustomed to, wrapped around her—and it felt good, and it felt right.

Edva snatched the carrot and pranced away, leaving Phe smiling after her.

Roar tapped her forearm, drawing Phe's gaze there. His touch walked the fence between relief and discomfort. "Is there a meaning behind Edva?"

Phe blinked at him, her heart rate picking up. "Behind Edva? Hmm." Phe looked up and to the right, playfully pensive. It was as if by magic the name had come to her. It was a name she'd never considered, nor had she heard before, yet it felt perfect for the foal's spirit and personality. "Beyond the fact she actually accepted a name, it fits her. Edvas are bold and bullheaded and filled with unwavering willpower alongside their fiery spirit."

Roar laughed. "Did you make that up?"

Phe shrugged, her gaze wandering to Edva. "Maybe."

What had her heart thumping with radiant joy was that all of Edva's feistiness was hers to love.

EPILOGUE II

Phe breathed through her mouth in slow, measured breaths and pressed her back into the moist, smooth stone wall of Brinehold's jail. Its chill seeped past the barrier of her twin's sheaths and leather clothing, grounding her unsteady heartbeat—her spiraling mind—as she watched Seskel sleep.

His face was angled toward the hallway entrance, half covered by two heavy blankets. She marveled at how relaxed, how deeply—how contentedly—he slept. Like a man with no soul.

Do I look like that too?

The moment the thought manifested, she shrugged it off. They were different types of monsters entirely, for now. But—she swallowed hard—maybe that would change tonight? Maybe, if she did what she'd come here to do every night since she could walk again, she'd become a little more like him.

Ruthless.

Selfish.

Despicable.

Her heart scoffed an *as-if* at her. One she silently mimicked, because it was right. She'd be lying to herself if she thought killing Seskel tonight would be the cure to her tortured soul. It wouldn't.

The cold pulled at her, bringing her back into the shadowed corner she leaned in. Instinctively, she reached for the shadows, imagining wrapping them in layers around herself and refocusing on *him*.

Everything she saw—his private cell tower, the blankets, the raised pallet, the clean, working toilet, the fresh air—ignited sparks of festering rage, filling her lungs with its gaseous poison. Making it hard to breathe. Reminding her what privilege looked like, even in Brinehold, the facility that held everyone awaiting trial or punishment in Oceanid.

Like each night she'd been here before, she gripped the pommels of her thigh knives, and closed her eyes. On her inhale, she imagined herself quietly unlocking the cell and striding in. She imagined tossing his blankets aside, jabbing her knee into his back, fisting her hand into his hair, and yanking his neck toward her as painfully as possible. Making eye contact and smiling, letting him see her for who she really is—showing him Lady's Orphne's secret—as she caressed his face with her knife.

Running it along the same path he took on hers.

Phe dragged in a tense breath, opened her eyes, and banished the images. Banished the darkness it danced with. Softly, she traced the path Seskel had carved into her own face until they rested on her lips. The now smooth skin throbbed.

She dropped her hand, and by the time it rested at her side, she was unsure if she'd fisted it or if it had curled itself.

Should I kill him?

It was the same question she'd asked herself every visit.

Yet, tonight was different.

Tonight was the last night he would be in Xafara.

Seskel's breath caught, as if he'd heard her thoughts, and his body tensed. One of his blankets slid to the floor.

Her lips twisted into a gnarly branch.

Crooked. Brittle. Jagged.

I wouldn't be in this position if it weren't for Bastion.

Phe ground her teeth as a wave of blistering anger swept through her, scorching her neck and chest. She let her head tip backwards, resting it against the wall. It wasn't just Bastion's fault. No, that would be too easy. It went deeper. Wider. It was the entire justice system—Xafara's proud, polished illusion of order and equality.

For those without connections or wealth, there was no mercy.

No leniency.

Only judgment—swift and brutal.

But for the connected?

For families like Seskel's?

Easements were had. Rules bent. And, punishments mere formalities. Consequences in name only—something to calm the public.

The memory hit like a gavel.

Suddenly, she was back in the courtroom—a moment she'd been reliving too often.

The hard planes of the glossy oak seat of Xafara's courtroom made Phe shift uncomfortably. The dress Phe wore felt too tight, too heavy, for Phe... but it was perfect for Lady Orphne. *She* needed the weight to feel safe. Like a tether. Without it, *her* mind might drift into the darkness Phe'd clawed her way out of, and its weight countered the pulsing anxiety skittering through her veins and tormenting her stomach.

Phe—or rather, Lady Orphne—kept her chin tilted downward, steady as stone. Phe wanted to look away, scan the crowd. Lady Orphne wouldn't let her. Anticipation clung to the air—dense and tense. It tasted of rindra root: sour, bitter, and strong enough to make her throat tighten. Stirring her nausea.

Kyra flung a hand outward, animatedly talking in her singsong way to Isri, one of the parliament member's daughters—and a long-standing friend of the Brevil family.

Lady Orphne flinched. Kyra didn't notice.

Isri had been one of the hundreds who packed the courtroom for Seskel's trial, loudly advocating for his innocence. The sight of her—of them—made Phe and Lady Orphne's insides twist.

Lady Orphne curled into herself, making herself smaller.

Phe pressed her leg into the side of the seat, feeling the edge of her thigh knife and sheath dig into her. Reminding her, she may be Lady Orphne now. Weak, sick, cowering, but Phe existed beneath the mask. Lady Orphne was trembling. But, Phe was the one holding the knife. Waiting. Like a switch she could flip at any moment. Reminding her, she was powerful. That she was a shield—not just for Kyra, but for the ones she'd helped save.

The ones who hadn't been spared.

Under the cover of her lashes, she glanced at Seskel and immediately shuddered when they made eye contact. She dropped her gaze, but not fast enough to have noticed he was casually twisted in his seat, holding his own court with his family and team, smiling amidst a round of laughter.

Gads, she despised him.

Why had they sat here—*almost directly behind him*—where his gaze could drift to her almost unnoticeably?

Because Isri had spotted Kyra the moment they entered the courtroom for the verdict and steered her to this seat. And Kyra, not noticing who sat in front of them at first, followed without question— simply unaware until it was too late.

Even though everyone knew.

Everyone.

About Seskel's obsession.

Phe didn't blame Kyra. But the ache settled anyway, like it always did.

Maybe it was Phe's ultra-aware senses. Or maybe it was Lady Orphne, scanning the air like prey always does—sensing the shift before anyone else. Maybe it was the way the air tightened, growing heavier, tinged with something tart. But she knew the moment Bastion's hand touched the doorknob. The noise in the room dulled as her focus locked on the door. Watched the knob twist, the door ease open, and Bastion step through.

Her fingers tightened around each other when his brown gaze pierced hers and held for a moment that felt like a minute, flicking to Kyra, Isri, then landing, unwaveringly, on Seskel.

Phe watched the scar on his face tighten with whatever he'd seen and not liked. Lady Orphne shrunk an inch into her seat. It was probably something about her.

Bastion took the podium while the rest, filing in behind him, settled into their respective seats. From Phe's periphery, she watched Seskel straighten and tension plunge into the muscles of his back. Phe's heart cracked a smile.

Suddenly, silence suffocated the room.

Silence Bastion basked in as his gaze roamed the overflowing crowd.

When the air was so thick it felt hard to breathe, Bastion announced. "Seskel Brevil, you have been found guilty of . . ."

The room erupted in noise, drowning out the list of Seskel's crimes.

"Silence!" Bastion's voice commanded, and instantly, there was.

"Your criminal activities extended beyond the boundaries of Xafara, as such, your punishment reflects this." Bastion continued, unaffected by the thickening apprehension filling the room.

"After careful deliberation and in cooperation with the authorities of Shalexum, you are to be extradited immediately and exiled from Xafara."

Lady Orphne listened, unmoving, while tears of blood pooled inside her.

"There, you will stand trial for the crimes you committed on their soil."

The room relaxed. But not Phe. She felt his verdict—sharp, sudden, like a blow to the gut.

How could they?

Shalexum allowed human trafficking. Sending Seskel there meant he wouldn't be punished. His family would get him set up, support him, and he'd keep on hurting people. Killing people.

Lady Orphne lost feeling in her limbs. Her heart.

How could the bastard allow them to agree to this punishment? He was there when they rescued people from Seabreak Orphanage.

Bastion paused, drilling Phe with his gaze. "Seskel Brevil, you'll face whatever justice is seen fit by those entrusted with the task."

Grimly, Bastion's gaze speared the crowd, holding a promise of pain Phe was very familiar with. "Let it be known—Xafara was built on law, not lineage. And under that law, every citizen is entitled to the same rights, held to the same standards."

He let the silence settle, deliberate and weighted.

"It is not wealth that protects you. Not your name. Not your father's position."

His voice rang clear through the stillness.

"Justice belongs to the people. To the wronged. And to those who can no longer speak for themselves." Another pause—longer this time, sharper, like the edge of a drawn blade. "Today, we sentence the ringleader."

He let that hang.

"Tomorrow, we go after the ring."

He didn't move. Not yet.

His gaze swept the courtroom—cold, calculating, accusatory, and unblinking.

Silence reigned, thick and brittle. No one dared to breathe.

Only when the tension had stretched to a breaking point did Bastion finally turn and stride out.

Phe collapsed into the seat, not realizing she'd been leaning forward or that her heart was fluttering wildly, erratically. That was Lady Orphne—reeling, faint, sick with betrayal. But beneath her trembling frame, Phe seethed.

How could he say all that and send Seskel to Shalexum?

At Bastion's exit, Seskel stood and fell into the open arms of his parents. His smile devoured his whole face, and those eyes of his . . . they found her—brimming with vile hunger.

A fresh coat of sweat broke—Lady Orphne's panic, not hers, clinging like a borrowed shroud. And she wasn't sure she had the strength to stand without fainting. Not with the roar of betrayal thundering through her. Not with the knee-buckling grief—for the survivors, for the lost—that justice hadn't come. Not with the monster erupting from the cavity of her chest—bellowing and demanding retribution. Demanding Phe be the hand of justice.

It wasn't until Kyra cradled her face—her touch sparking discomfort, her green gaze filling Lady Orphne's vision, her voice calm and steady saying, "Breathe with me, Phe"—that she realized she'd been gasping for air.

The damp, grimy air of the jail scraped down her throat, dragging her back to the present.

To the chill of stone of Brinehold. To the stench of sweat and the undertones of unwashed bodies and fear.

To the monstrous voice, still bellowing; *kill him.*

Phe scrubbed her face with her hands, feeling the filth grind against her skin—and wondered if that was what her soul looked like. Filthy. Stained.

With all the things she'd done—all the killing—no matter how she justified it, hadn't it marked her? Had this been how Grum started too? Killing to survive? Killing to protect the ones he'd loved?

Phe shook her head to clear it and strode to the lock on his door and crouched, pulling free her tools. Even though she hadn't decided to kill Seskel, she'd found over the nights she'd visited him there was something achingly satisfying to stand over his sleeping form knowing she could end him at any moment.

"You're almost there." Grum chuckled—softly, mockingly. *"You always thought you were different. Better."* His hot breath curdled the hairs on her nape. *"But now look at you... walking my path."* Glee laced every word.

Phe closed her eyes and gritted her teeth. *Stars.* If she did this. . . what would make her different from *Grum*? She knew killing Seskel would carry different consequences. That it would stir the beast within her, make it hunger for more retribution—neatly justified as *justice.*

Phe leaned her head against the cool metal, needing to pause. Needing to let those questions wash over her, again, as they had every night she'd visited. But, at least those nights, Grum's shadow presence had remained blissfully silent until now.

She gritted her teeth. That voice—his voice—wasn't him. Not

anymore. Just what he'd left behind. Just what he'd left rotting in her mind.

She imagined folding him up. Word by word. Breath by breath. Stuffing the voice into a box lined with fire and shadows, then slamming the lid. Sealing it. Shoving it into the farthest, blackest corner of her mind.

Her skin prickled—an electric awareness crawling up her arms and down her spine.

She wasn't alone.

She didn't need to look. She just knew.

It was a knowing stitched into her bones—the kind that had always told her where people were, and who they were.

A knowing that had helped keep her alive.

And right now, the one person she least wanted near her was standing behind her.

Silent. Unannounced. Appearing out of nowhere—like magic.

Stars, why him? *Why right now?*

Giving the lock an *I-promise-I'll-be-back* look, she pushed away from the cell, still on her haunches, away from Bastion's prying eyes. Slowly, she straightened to her height and angled herself toward her shadows.

She didn't need to look to know he was there. Casual. Watching. Standing in the doorway like he'd been there the whole time. And, she wanted nothing more than to banish his existence into the farthest galaxy. Instead, she forced herself to ask, her voice rough enough to take off a layer of his skin. "Why are you here?"

Seskel jerked upright, his blankets pooling at his hips.

"I was wondering what you'd do," Bastion replied in a neutral tone—one that was completely out of character for him to be using toward her.

Suspicion stung Phe's nose as if she'd inhaled something spicy, and her anger . . . her smoldering, barely contained anger at him, at Seskel, at the system, detonated. She bit into her inner cheek, hard, and began her count. *"One, two, three..."* Inhaling deeply with each number and forcefully relaxing the lines of her face, so that by the time she faced Bastion, the only tell of violence she had was the fire in her eyes.

She let her silence answer, fuming at his question. *He* was wondering what *she* would do?

"What's happening?" Seskel asked, his voice groggy. Groggy and entirely too unconcerned for Phe's liking.

"Four, five, six, seven..." Phe slid her lock-picking tool into its tiny pocket, then hooked her thumbs onto the pommels of her thigh knives, loose. Ready. The metal felt decadent in her grasp, cooling her heat, melting the red-tinging her vision, and reminding her who she is: A warrior. A survivor.

When she met Bastion's gaze, he gestured toward Seskel. "Please, don't let me stop you."

Phe huffed an *as-if-you-could* response. If she wanted him dead, he'd be dead.

"General Bastion?" Seskel continued, moving off his pallet toward them. "What's the meaning of this?"

"Eight, nine, ten." If looks could obliterate people, Seskel would not be sharing air with Phe, or with anyone else in Aethra. Dismissing him, she returned to her thoughts. Why was Bastion here? He never paid any interest to her unless it was to train or cause her pain. And his tone . . . he was being *decent*? Why did he care what she did to Seskel?

"Lady Orphne?" This time, Seskel's pitch hit the ceiling, shock cascading through his expression.

"Well..." Bastion coaxed.

She suppressed a shudder at having to hear both their voices. Of course, it made sense, somewhere in the distant stars or depths of the sea, that the two people she despised the most would be talking, at the same time, in the same room as her.

But she knew, without a doubt, Bastion would not let her leave unless she answered him. And the worst part, it wasn't a one and done. He'd talk back.

Sighing audibly, her tone clearly telling Bastion how unimpressed she was at having to even interact with him, she said. "I haven't decided yet."

"No?" Bastion questioned in a tone that made Phe want to punch him. Instead, she tightened her grip on her pommels, stealing their strength and resolve. "Seems pretty obvious."

Phe pinned Bastion with a scowl. "If that were the case, he'd have been dead long ago."

"You've been coming nightly?" Bastion stepped further into the room, his eyes catching something in her—maybe the quiet war. Maybe the restraint. Maybe the ache. Whatever it was, it flashed in his gaze, then vanished a breath later.

Phe tracked his movement. He stepped in—three steps. Closer than she liked. Then, again, him being with her right now was closer than she liked. But, he wasn't close enough to be a threat. Yet.

She tugged the shadows at her ankles closer and leaned into the chilly rock wall. "Since I could walk again."

"How close have you gotten?"

Irritation crackled in her stare, answering for her.

"This is unlike you," Bastion stated the obvious.

Stars, she didn't need him to tell her that. She *knew*.

"Have you come to protect him?" She asked.

"Protect me from what?" Seskel asked, gripping the bars of his cell. "I don't understand what's happening."

"No," Bastion replied.

Phe grunted, "Then why are you here?"

"I have my reasons." He didn't acknowledge Seskel. His focus was still all on her. "What's the barrier?"

The words struck her like a match.

Because if I do... I'll prove Grum right.

Because if I do... I'll become what he said I was. What he made me.

But she didn't say that. She couldn't. She wouldn't give Grum's ghost the satisfaction, nor Bastion the leverage.

Switching topics, she let bitterness ride her words. "Help me understand. How is sending him to Shalexum punishing him? What kind of message do you think you've sent Xafarian's?"

"Intolerance."

Phe's laugh tasted sour, "The message I heard was if your family has enough money and influence, you'll be exiled to a life of privilege and luxury and freedom to keep on doing what you were doing, but only now, you're doing it in a country that allows it."

"A cage can look like freedom if you don't know what to look for," Bastion said, his voice measured—and again, she was struck by the lack of bite. No barbs, no coldness. Just... words. It was like Bastion was talking to a member of Shadow Unit. Not her. And somehow, that unsettled her more. "And sometimes... justice can appear to wear the face of mercy." His gaze flicked to her. "You, of all people, know that."

Tides knew she did.

It was the story of her life. Moving from one cage to another. But, what did that have to do with Seskel? He wasn't being caged.

"What about Oriana and all the victims?" Phe's voice sliced sharply at him. "What about all the others? You talk about justice, but how is this anything close? His punishment isn't comparable to what they endured. Have you found everyone he sent to Shalexum? Do you even know what happens there?"

The memory struck before she could shove it away—cheering voices, a stadium packed with bodies, the oppressive heat rising off the arena sands. The thick, cloying stench of blood.

No. She refused to go back there.

Her jaw tightened as she blinked hard, shoving it where it belonged—back into the box it had clawed its way out of, deep inside her.

She was here.

She'd survived.

That was then. This was now.

Even if her past still bled into the now.

"I'm not dignifying that with a response," Bastion curtly replied, shutting Phe down—giving her a pinch of his usual, belligerent self. "Why haven't you killed him?"

Seskel let out a forced laugh, the sound hollow. "She can't kill me."

Phe licked her dry lips, debating telling him. It wasn't like he didn't know some of her driving demons. Bastion was her nemesis. Yet, he also knew her—knew her well. Years of training would do that.

Bastion's jaw tightened—a flicker of impatience.

"No," Seskel's voice rose, still strained. "There's no way."

Phe's response was low but steady. "Because it's not an order."

Bastion shrugged, his indifference relieving. "Is that all?"

She shook her head, no, and pressed her teeth into her lip, sealing her mouth. Grum snickered in the recesses of her mind, *"Too late for that, little monster."*

The words shot up before she could stop them—bursting from her like a cork blown off a bottle, the pressure too high, the silence held too long.

"I don't want to be like him."

"Like me?" Seskel asked.

"Grum," Bastion stated.

Phe's skin crawled at the sound of his name. And she hated that Bastion knew her well enough to use it like a weapon—just saying it was a strike.

"Yes, *Grum*." The name tasted like rust and bile—corrosive, sour with nightmarish memory. "I don't want to turn into *him*." *Become more of a monster.* "Someone who thinks they can exact their own justice, control, or power. If I kill those I've decided wronged me or others, the killing will never end."

Bastion's gaze flickered with something. It looked almost like approval for a moment, but it was gone as quickly as it had appeared.

"Lady Orphne, what are you *wearing*? And who is Grum?" Seskel demanded, irritation riding his tone. "What is the meaning of this?"

Phe would never tell Bastion she already considered herself a monster. How could she not? She'd survived Grum by doing unspeakable things—even if they were forced. She'd followed Bastion's orders and left a trail of bodies behind—all for Kyra.

There was no clean version of her. There never had been.

But she told herself it wasn't all darkness. Not yet. Maybe she was still just a baby beast—one with purpose. With boundaries.

If she did this... if she killed for her own justice—not for survival, not out of duty—she wouldn't be a baby anymore. She'd grow teeth. And she wasn't sure she'd ever stop.

"Sometimes," Bastion said quietly, his voice softening into a tone she hadn't heard in a decade. Not since she was young. And even then, it had been rare—like a kindness he didn't quite know how to hold.

The shift threw her. She'd rather face his barbed tongue or blood in the air. And for a moment, she considered provoking exactly that.

"Doing what's necessary means making choices that don't align with your values."

Her eyes narrowed, defiance flaring. "If going against our values is what it takes to uphold justice, what's right, what's decent, then we've already lost."

Bastion said nothing. Silence stretched between them, weighted with unsaid truths.

The truth hit hard—fast and final, like a blade to the sternum.

She'd built her life on one vow: outside of orders and protecting Kyra, she didn't hurt people.

If she killed Seskel now—not to protect, not to survive, but to punish—she'd break that.

She already carried the baby beast. And Grum—always Grum— still lingered at the edges, whispering, gnawing at what was left of her soul.

She didn't need to feed them a feast.

She straightened, slow and deliberate, spine stacking one vertebra at a time. The decision wasn't just made. It was worn now— like armor. Shadow armor.

Bastion grimly smiled. "I see you've made your decision."

"What decision?" Seskel questioned tensely.

"I have." Phe acknowledged.

With a curt nod, Bastion paused. The air between them shifted—

denser, colder—before his gaze sliced into Seskel like a sword. "Don't mistake exile for a reward. One way or another, justice finds its own path."

Phe swallowed, the meaning behind his words pressing against her ribs. Bastion never made empty promises. And he wasn't making one now.

Being exiled to Shalexum seemed to be a reward, not a punishment—but Bastion's tone suggested otherwise. He was telling her something without saying it outright.

That Seskel wouldn't walk away from this untouched.

That exile wasn't the freedom it appeared to be.

As usual, he told her nothing. A handful of words, loaded pauses —breadcrumbs instead of answers. At least this time, she didn't mind the message.

She shot Seskel one last glance, memorizing him—not as a lingering threat, but as a reminder. Justice was coming. She didn't know how, and she didn't need to.

She trusted Bastion to handle the mission. The outcome. The optics.

She just didn't trust him with her.

That trust—limited as it was—wasn't the point.

This was her choice. Her control.

That was the point of this moment. Of her moment.

To choose who she became—not who they made her.

Because walking away wasn't a weakness. It was proof.

Proof that she was more than what Grum made. More than the blade Bastion sharpened. And maybe... maybe being spared wasn't just about surviving. Maybe it was about being shaped into something more. A path that, despite its pain, hadn't just saved her—it had prepared her.Phe breathed through her mouth in slow, measured breaths and pressed her back into the moist, smooth stone wall of Brinehold's jail. Its chill seeped past the barrier of her twin's sheaths and leather clothing, grounding her unsteady heartbeat—her spiraling mind—as she watched Seskel sleep.

His face was angled toward the hallway entrance, half covered by two heavy blankets. She marveled at how relaxed, how deeply—how contentedly—he slept. Like a man with no soul.

Do I look like that too?

The moment the thought manifested, she shrugged it off. They were different types of monsters entirely, for now. But—she swallowed hard—maybe that would change tonight? Maybe, if she did what she'd come here to do every night since she could walk again, she'd become a little more like him.

Ruthless.

Selfish.

Despicable.

Her heart scoffed an *as-if* at her. One she silently mimicked, because it was right. She'd be lying to herself if she thought killing Seskel tonight would be the cure to her tortured soul. It wouldn't.

The cold pulled at her, bringing her back into the shadowed corner she leaned in. Instinctively, she reached for the shadows, imagining wrapping them in layers around herself and refocusing on *him*.

Everything she saw—his private cell tower, the blankets, the raised pallet, the clean, working toilet, the fresh air—ignited sparks of festering rage, filling her lungs with its gaseous poison. Making it hard to breathe. Reminding her what privilege looked like, even in Brinehold, the facility that held everyone awaiting trial or punishment in Oceanid.

Like each night she'd been here before, she gripped the pommels of her thigh knives, and closed her eyes. On her inhale, she imagined herself quietly unlocking the cell and striding in. She imagined tossing his blankets aside, jabbing her knee into his back, fisting her hand into his hair, and yanking his neck toward her as painfully as possible. Making eye contact and smiling, letting him see her for who she really is—showing him Lady's Orphne's secret—as she caressed his face with her knife.

Running it along the same path he took on hers.

Phe dragged in a tense breath, opened her eyes, and banished the images. Banished the darkness it danced with. Softly, she traced the path Seskel had carved into her own face until they rested on her lips. The now smooth skin throbbed.

She dropped her hand, and by the time it rested at her side, she was unsure if she'd fisted it or if it had curled itself.

Should I kill him?

It was the same question she'd asked herself every visit.

Yet, tonight was different.

Tonight, was the last night he would be in Xafara.

Seskel's breath caught, as if he'd heard her thoughts, and his body tensed. One of his blankets slid to the floor.

Her lips twisted into a gnarly branch.

Crooked. Brittle. Jagged.

I wouldn't be in this position if it weren't for Bastion.

Phe ground her teeth as a wave of blistering anger swept through her, scorching her neck and chest. She let her head tip backwards, resting it against the wall. It wasn't just Bastion's fault. No, that would be too easy. It went deeper. Wider. It was the entire justice system— Xafara's proud, polished illusion of order and equality.

For those without connections or wealth, there was no mercy.

No leniency.

Only judgment—swift and brutal.

But for the connected?

For families like Seskel's?

Easements were had. Rules bent. And, punishments mere formalities. Consequences in name only—something to calm the public.

The memory hit like a gavel.

Suddenly, she was back in the courtroom—a moment she'd been reliving too often.

The hard planes of the glossy oak seat of Xafara's courtroom made Phe shift uncomfortably. The dress Phe wore felt too tight, too heavy, for Phe... but it was perfect for Lady Orphne. *She* needed the weight to feel safe. Like a tether. Without it, *her* mind might drift into the darkness Phe'd clawed her way out of, and its weight countered the pulsing anxiety skittering through her veins and tormenting her stomach.

Phe—or rather, Lady Orphne—kept her chin tilted downward, steady as stone. Phe wanted to look away, scan the crowd. Lady Orphne wouldn't let her. Anticipation clung to the air—dense and tense. It tasted of rindra root: sour, bitter, and strong enough to make her throat tighten. Stirring her nausea.

Kyra flung a hand outward, animatedly talking in her singsong way to Isri, one of the parliament member's daughters—and a long-standing friend of the Brevil family.

Lady Orphne flinched. Kyra didn't notice.

Isri had been one of the hundreds who packed the courtroom for Seskel's trial, loudly advocating for his innocence. The sight of her—of them—made Phe and Lady Orphne's insides twist.

Lady Orphne curled into herself, making herself smaller.

Phe pressed her leg into the side of the seat, feeling the edge of her thigh knife and sheath dig into her. Reminding her, she maybe Lady Orphne now. Weak, sick, cowering, but Phe existed beneath the mask. Lady Orphne was trembling. But, Phe was the one holding the knife. Waiting. Like a switch she could flip at any moment. Reminding her, she was powerful. That she was a shield—not just for Kyra, but for the ones she'd helped save.

The ones who hadn't been spared.

Under the cover of her lashes, she glanced at Seskel and immediately shuddered when they made eye contact. She dropped her gaze, but not fast enough to have noticed he was causally twisted in his seat, holding his own court with his family and team, smiling amidst a round of laughter.

Gads, she despised him.

Why had they sat here—*almost directly behind him*—where his gaze could drift to her almost unnoticeably?

Because Isri had spotted Kyra the moment they entered the courtroom for the verdict and steered her to this seat. And Kyra, not noticing who sat in front of them at first, followed without question—simply unaware until it was too late.

Even though everyone knew.

Everyone.

About Seskel's obsession.

Phe didn't blame Kyra. But the ache settled anyway, like it always did.

Maybe it was Phe's ultra-aware senses. Or maybe it was Lady Orphne, scanning the air like prey always does—sensing the shift before anyone else. Maybe it was the way the air tightened, growing heavier, tinged with something tart. But she knew the moment Bastion's hand touched the doorknob. The noise in the room dulled as her focus locked on the door. Watched the knob twist, the door ease open, and Bastion step through.

Her fingers tightened around each other when his brown gaze pierced hers and held for a moment that felt like a minute, flicking to Kyra, Isri, then landing, unwaveringly, on Seskel.

Phe watched the scar on his face tighten with whatever he'd seen and not liked. Lady Orphne shrunk an inch into her seat. It was probably something about her.

Bastion took the podium while the rest, filing in behind him, settled into their respective seats. From Phe's periphery, she watched Seskel straighten and tension plunge into the muscles of his back. Phe's heart cracked a smile.

Suddenly, silence suffocated the room.

Silence Bastion basked in as his gaze roamed the overflowing crowd.

When the air was so thick it felt hard to breathe, Bastion announced. "Seskel Brevil, you have been found guilty of . . ."

The room erupted in noise, drowning out the list of Seskel's crimes.

"Silence!" Bastion's voice commanded, and instantly, there was.

"Your criminal activities extended beyond the boundaries of Xafara, as such, your punishment reflects this." Bastion continued, unaffected by the thickening apprehension filling the room.

"After careful deliberation and in cooperation with the authorities of Shalexum, you are to be extradited immediately and exiled from Xafara."

Lady Orphne listened, unmoving, while tears of blood pooled inside her.

"There, you will stand trial for the crimes you committed on their soil."

The room relaxed. But not Phe. She felt his verdict—sharp, sudden, like a blow to the gut.

How could they?

Shalexum allowed human trafficking. Sending Seskel there meant he wouldn't be punished. His family would get him set up, support him, and he'd keep on hurting people. Killing people.

Lady Orphne lost feeling in her limbs. Her heart.

How could the bastard allow them to agree to this punishment? He was there when they rescued people from Seabreak Orphanage.

Bastion paused, drilling Phe with his gaze. "Seskel Brevil, you'll face whatever justice is seen fit by those entrusted with the task."

Grimly, Bastion's gaze speared the crowd, holding a promise of pain Phe was very familiar with. "Let it be known—Xafara was built on law, not lineage. And under that law, every citizen is entitled to the same rights, held to the same standards."

He let the silence settle, deliberate and weighted.

"It is not wealth that protects you. Not your name. Not your father's position."

His voice rang clear through the stillness.

"Justice belongs to the people. To the wronged. And to those who can no longer speak for themselves." Another pause—longer this time, sharper, like the edge of a drawn blade. "Today, we sentence the ringleader."

He let that hang.

"Tomorrow, we go after the ring."

He didn't move. Not yet.

His gaze swept the courtroom—cold, calculating, accusatory, and unblinking.

Silence reigned, thick and brittle. No one dared to breathe.

Only when the tension had stretched to a breaking point did Bastion finally turn and stride out.

Phe collapsed into the seat, not realizing she'd been leaning forward or that her heart was fluttering wildly, erratically. That was Lady Orphne—reeling, faint, sick with betrayal. But beneath her trembling frame, Phe seethed.

How could he say all that and send Seskel to Shalexum?

At Bastion's exit, Seskel stood and fell into the open arms of his parents. His smile devoured his whole face, and those eyes of his . . . they found her—brimming with vile hunger.

A fresh coat of sweat broke—Lady Orphne's panic, not hers, clinging like a borrowed shroud. And she wasn't sure she had the strength to stand without fainting. Not with the roar of betrayal thundering through her. Not with the knee-buckling grief—for the survivors, for the lost—that justice hadn't come. Not with the monster erupting from the cavity of her chest—bellowing and demanding retribution. Demanding Phe be the hand of justice.

It wasn't until Kyra cradled her face—her touch sparking discomfort, her green gaze filling Lady Orphne's vision, her voice calm and steady saying, "Breathe with me, Phe"—that she realized she'd been gasping for air.

The damp, grimy air of the jail scraped down her throat, dragging her back to the present.

To the chill of stone of Brinehold. To the stench of sweat and the undertones of unwashed bodies and fear.

To the monstrous voice, still bellowing; *kill him.*

Phe scrubbed her face with her hands, feeling the filth grind against her skin—and wondered if that was what her soul looked like. Filthy. Stained.

With all the things she'd done—all the killing—no matter how she justified it, hadn't it marked her? Had this been how Grum started too? Killing to survive? Killing to protect the ones he'd loved?

Phe shook her head to clear it and strode to the lock on his door and crouched, pulling free her tools. Even though she hadn't decided to kill Seskel, she'd found over the nights she'd visited him there was something achingly satisfying to stand over his sleeping form knowing she could end him at any moment.

"You're almost there." Grum chuckled—softly, mockingly. *"You always thought you were different. Better."* His hot breath curdled the hairs on her nape. *"But now look at you... walking my path."* Glee laced every word.

Phe closed her eyes and gritted her teeth. *Stars.* If she did this. . . what would make her different from *Grum*? She knew killing Seskel would carry different consequences. That it would stir the beast within her, make it hunger for more retribution—neatly justified as *justice.*

Phe leaned her head against the cool metal, needing to pause. Needing to let those questions wash over her, again, as they had every night she'd visited. But, at least those nights, Grum's shadow presence had remained blissfully silent until now.

She gritted her teeth. That voice—his voice—wasn't him. Not anymore. Just what he'd left behind. Just what he'd left rotting in her mind.

She imagined folding him up. Word by word. Breath by breath. Stuffing the voice into a box lined with fire and shadows, then slamming the lid. Sealing it. Shoving it into the farthest, blackest corner of her mind.

Her skin prickled—an electric awareness crawling up her arms and down her spine.

She wasn't alone.

She didn't need to look. She just knew.

It was a knowing stitched into her bones—the kind that had always told her where people were, and who they were.

A knowing that had helped keep her alive.

And right now, the one person she least wanted near her was standing behind her.

Silent. Unannounced. Appearing out of nowhere—like magic.

Stars, why him? *Why right now?*

Giving the lock a *I-promise-I'll-be-back* look, she pushed away from the cell, still on her haunches, away from Bastion's prying eyes. Slowly, she straightened to her height and angled herself toward her shadows.

She didn't need to look to know he was there. Casual. Watching. Standing in the doorway like he'd been there the whole time. And, she wanted nothing more than to banish his existence into the farthest galaxy. Instead, she forced herself to ask, her voice rough enough to take off a layer of his skin. "Why are you here?"

Seskel jerked upright, his blankets pooling at his hips.

"I was wondering what you'd do," Bastion replied in a neutral tone—one that was completely out of character for him to be using toward her.

Suspicion stung Phe's nose as if she'd inhaled something spicy, and her anger . . . her smoldering, barely contained anger at him, at Seskel, at the system, detonated. She bit into her inner cheek, hard, and began her count. *"One, two, three..."* Inhaling deeply with each number and forcefully relaxing the lines of her face, so that by the time she faced Bastion, the only tell of violence she had was the fire in her eyes.

She let her silence answer, fuming at his question. *He* was wondering what *she* would do?

"What's happening?" Seskel asked, his voice groggy. Groggy and entirely too unconcerned for Phe's liking.

"Four, five, six, seven..." Phe slid her lock-picking tool into its tiny pocket, then hooked her thumbs onto the pommels of her thigh knives, loose. Ready. The metal felt decadent in her grasp, cooling her heat, melting the red-tinging her vision, and reminding her who she is. A warrior. A survivor.

When she met Bastion's gaze, he gestured toward Seskel. "Please, don't let me stop you."

Phe huffed an *as-if-you-could* response. If she wanted him dead, he'd be dead.

"General Bastion?" Seskel's continued, moving off his palette toward them. "What's the meaning of this?"

"Eight, nine, ten." If looks could obliterate people, Seskel would not be sharing air with Phe, or with anyone else in Aethra. Dismissing him, she returned to her thoughts. Why was Bastion here? He never paid any interest to her unless it was to train or cause her pain. And

his tone . . . he was being *decent*? Why did he care what she did to Seskel?

"Lady Orphne?" This time, Seskel's pitch hit the ceiling, shock cascading through his expression.

"Well..." Bastion coaxed.

She suppressed a shudder at having to hear both their voices. Of course, it made sense, somewhere in the distant stars or depths of the sea, that the two people she despised the most would be talking, at the same time, in the same room as her.

But she knew, without a doubt, Bastion would not let her leave unless she answered him. And the worst part, it wasn't a one and done. He'd talk back.

Sighing audibly, her tone clearly telling Bastion how unimpressed she was at having to even interact with him, she said. "I haven't decided yet."

"No?" Bastion questioned in a tone that made Phe want to punch him. Instead, she tightened her grip on her pommels, stealing their strength and resolve. "Seems pretty obvious."

Phe pinned Bastion with a scowl. "If that were the case, he'd have been dead long ago."

"You've been coming nightly?" Bastion stepped further into the room, his eyes catching something in her—maybe the quiet war. Maybe the restraint. Maybe the ache. Whatever it was, it flashed in his gaze, then vanished a breath later.

Phe tracked his movement. He stepped in—three steps. Closer than she liked. Then, again, him being with her right now was closer than she liked. But, he wasn't close enough to be a threat. Yet.

She tugged the shadows at her ankles closer and leaned into the chilly rock wall. "Since I could walk again."

"How close have you gotten?"

Irritation crackled in her stare, answering for her.

"This is unlike you," Bastion stated the obvious.

Stars, she didn't need him to tell her that. She *knew*.

"Have you come to protect him?" She asked.

"Protect me from what?" Seskel asked, gripping the bars of his cell. "I don't understand what's happening."

"No," Bastion replied.

Phe grunted, "Then why are you here?"

"I have my reasons." He didn't acknowledge Seskel. His focus was still all on her. "What's the barrier?"

The words struck her like a match.

Because if I do... I'll prove Grum right.

Because if I do... I'll become what he said I was. What he made me.

But she didn't say that. She couldn't. She wouldn't give Grum's ghost the satisfaction, nor Bastion the leverage.

Switching topics, she let bitterness ride her words. "Help me understand. How is sending him to Shalexum punishing him? What kind of message do you think you've sent Xafarian's?"

"Intolerance."

Phe's laugh tasted sour, "The message I heard was if your family has enough money and influence, you'll be exiled to a life of privilege and luxury and freedom to keep on doing what you were doing, but only now, you're doing it in a country that allows it."

"A cage can look like freedom if you don't know what to look for," Bastion said, his voice measured—and again, she was struck by the lack of bite. No barbs, no coldness. Just... words. It was like Bastion was talking to a member of Shadow Unit. Not her. And somehow, that unsettled her more. "And sometimes... justice can appear to wear the face of mercy." His gaze flicked to her. "You, of all people, know that."

Tides knew she did.

It was the story of her life. Moving from one cage to another. But, what did that have to do with Seskel? He wasn't being caged.

"What about Oriana and all the victims?" Phe's voice sliced sharply at him. "What about all the others? You talk about justice, but how is this anything close? His punishment isn't comparable to what they endured. Have you found everyone he sent to Shalexum? Do you even know what happens there?"

The memory struck before she could shove it away—cheering

voices, a stadium packed with bodies, the oppressive heat rising off the arena sands. The thick, cloying stench of blood.

No. She refused to go back there.

Her jaw tightened as she blinked hard, shoving it where it belonged—back into the box it had clawed its way out of, deep inside her.

She was here.

She'd survived.

That was then. This was now.

Even if her past still bled into the now.

"I'm not dignifying that with a response," Bastion curtly replied, shutting Phe down—giving her a pinch of his usual, belligerent self. "Why haven't you killed him?"

Seskel let out a forced laugh, the sound hollow. "She can't kill me."

Phe licked her dry lips, debating telling him. It wasn't like he didn't know some of her driving demons. Bastion was her nemesis. Yet, he also knew her—knew her well. Years of training would do that.

Bastion's jaw tightened—a flicker of impatience.

"No," Seskel's voice rose, still strained. "There's no way."

Phe's response was low but steady. "Because it's not an order."

Bastion shrugged, his indifference relieving. "Is that all?"

She shook her head, no, and pressed her teeth into her lip, sealing her mouth. Grum snickered in the recesses of her mind, *"Too late for that, little monster."*

The words clawed up before she could stop them—shotting from her like a cork blasted off a bottle, pressure too high, silence too long.

"I don't want to be like him."

"Like me?" Seskel asked.

"Grum," Bastion stated.

Phe's skin crawled at the sound of his name. And she hated that Bastion knew her well enough to use it like a weapon—just saying it was a strike.

"Yes, *Grum*." The name tasted like rust and bile—corrosive, sour with nightmarish memory. "I don't want to turn into *him*." *Become more of a monster.* "Someone who thinks they can exact their own justice, control, or power. If I kill those I've decided wronged me or others, the killing will never end."

Bastion's gaze flickered with something. It looked almost like approval for a moment, but it was gone as quickly as it had appeared.

"Lady Orphne, what are you *wearing*? And who is Grum?" Seskel demanded, irritation riding his tone. "What is the meaning of this?"

Phe would never tell Bastion she already considered herself a monster. How could she not? She'd survived Grum by doing unspeakable things—even if they were forced. She'd followed Bastion's orders and left a trail of bodies behind—all for Kyra.

There was no clean version of her. There never had been.

But she told herself it wasn't all darkness. Not yet. Maybe she was still just a baby beast—one with purpose. With boundaries.

If she did this... if she killed for her own justice—not for survival, not out of duty—she wouldn't be a baby anymore. She'd grow teeth. And she wasn't sure she'd ever stop.

"Sometimes," Bastion said quietly, his voice softening into a tone she hadn't heard in a decade. Not since she was young. And even then, it had been rare—like a kindness he didn't quite know how to hold.

The shift threw her. She'd rather face his barbed tongue or blood in the air. And for a moment, she considered provoking exactly that.

"Doing what's necessary means making choices that don't align with your values."

Her eyes narrowed, defiance flaring. "If going against our values is what it takes to uphold justice, what's right, what's decent, then we've already lost."

Bastion said nothing. Silence stretched between them, weighted with unsaid truths.

The truth hit hard—fast and final, like a blade to the sternum.

She'd built her life on one vow: outside of orders and protecting Kyra, she didn't hurt people.

If she killed Seskel now—not to protect, not to survive, but to punish—she'd break that.

She already carried the baby beast. And Grum—always Grum— still lingered at the edges, whispering, gnawing at what was left of her soul.

She didn't need to feed them a feast.

She straightened, slow and deliberate, spine stacking one vertebra at a time. The decision wasn't just made. It was worn now— like armor. Shadow armor.

Bastion grimly smiled. "I see you've made your decision."

"What decision?" Seskel questioned tensely.

"I have." Phe acknowledged.

With a curt nod, Bastion paused. The air between them shifted— denser, colder—before his gaze sliced into Seskel like a sword. "Don't mistake exile for a reward. One way or another, justice finds its own path."

Phe swallowed, the meaning behind his words pressing against her ribs. Bastion never made empty promises. And he wasn't making one now.

Being exiled to Shalexum seemed to be a reward, not a punishment—but Bastion's tone suggested otherwise. He was telling her something without saying it outright.

That Seskel wouldn't walk away from this untouched.

That exile wasn't the freedom it appeared to be.

As usual, he told her nothing. A handful of words, loaded pauses —breadcrumbs instead of answers. At least this time, she didn't mind the message.

She shot Seskel one last glance, memorizing him—not as a lingering threat, but as a reminder. Justice was coming. She didn't know how, and she didn't need to.

She trusted Bastion to handle the mission. The outcome. The optics.

She just didn't trust him with her.

That trust—limited as it was—wasn't the point.

This was her choice. Her control.

That was the point of this moment. Of her moment.

To choose who she became—not who they made her.

Because walking away wasn't a weakness. It was proof.

Proof that she was more than what Grum made. More than the blade Bastion sharpened. And maybe... maybe being spared wasn't just about surviving. Maybe it was about being shaped into something more. A path that, despite its pain, hadn't just saved her—it had prepared her.

Phe exhaled, letting the truth settle like weight across her shoulders.

Then she brushed by Bastion and disappeared into the dark hallway of Brinehold.

For now, that would have to be enough.

AFTERWORD

This is a fictitious story created around fictitious characters depicting something that, unfortunately, is currently happening in too many lives.

I have portrayed sex trafficking in the most societally acknowledged way, where people are kidnapped and forced to into trafficking situations. It is viewed as rare and heinous and for a specific black-market clientele and not in our communities.

Yet, the fact is, sexual—human—trafficking happens all the time. In plain sight and out of it.

At motels, hotels, truck stops, street corners, in people's houses. With people you know.

It's a crime that touches infants, children, teenagers, adults, older adults, women and men. It is indiscriminate.

It's an industry where people are bought and sold across the US and the world, by family, partners, gangs, and traffickers. It's an industry that on one end meets the black-market stereotype, then stretches into backyards (from rural communities to high-end ones), from trucks and cars to airplanes and luxury hotels.

Some victims go missing, while others have to try to act normal around peers and teachers and family and co-workers.

From my experience in the mental health field, trauma symptoms can present in drastically varied ways. Many become highly distracted, forgetful, some lash out in anger or aggression, some become socially withdrawn, begin to avoid eye contact, refuse to tell you wants going on, some gain weight, stop showering, become moody—can go from high to low rapidly, they may start using substances or self-harming. They may become suicidal.

If you are experiencing this or know/suspect someone who is, there are people waiting to take your call and help you on your road to recovery. Please call:

U.S. National Human Trafficking Hotline: 1-888-373-7888, Text "BeFree" 233733

National Domestic Violence Hotline: 800-799-7233, Text START to 88788

Suicide & Crisis Lifeline: Text or call 988

I have also, from my line of work, heard of story after story of survivors healing. Of living the lives they want, lives they create, and thriving in them. You can have this, too.

ABOUT THE AUTHOR

When Krysta Maravilla isn't squirrelled away writing, reading and eating Nutella, she can be found plotting her next adventure. With a passion for hiking and a desire to experience different cultures, she has lived in various places throughout the US and the world.

Her love of fantasy and adventure and romance has inspired her to write her own stories, which transport readers to fantastical worlds filled with magic and action where she weaves in themes of healing, friendship, and loyalty.

Sign up for Krysta Maravilla's newsletter if you want monthly updates on *Of Fire and Shadows* series, exclusive content—such as Shadow Tag a cut scene from Sunder, Book Two, her wanderings, and various projects.

Visit her online and subscribe at:
www.krystamaravilla.com

OF FIRE AND SHADOWS

Spark
Spared (A novella)

STAY MARVELOUS